Expectations
The Continuing Adventures
of a Young Cowboy

Stu Campbell

D1176614

NORTHERN PLAINS
PUBLIC LIBRARY
Ault, Colorado

This is a work of fiction.

ISBN: 978-0-9962019-1-9

6   5   4   3   2   1

Edited by Mira Perrizo
Cover and text design by D.K. Luraas
Cover painting by Larry Jones, Bouse, Arizona
Author photo by Elizabeth Dobbs

Printed in the United States of America

Contents

Four-Wheeler

The winter passed slowly. It got cold and stayed cold, although there wasn't much snow. Pat, Dwight, and I spent a lot of our time halter breaking the weaner colts. The halter breaking included teaching the colts how to lead, picking up their feet, saddling them with the kid's saddles and doing everything that they would be expected to do when they were bigger. Of course, they weren't big enough to start riding. We also halter broke Einstein and taught him to lead although he followed us around like a puppy. We didn't have any two-year-old colts to start riding. Other than feeding the replacement heifers and cows, and the weaner colts, there wasn't much to do.

We found ourselves finishing up early for the noon meal and supper and spent too much time in the kitchen drinking coffee and getting out of the cold. The cook didn't seem to mind, but I thought we might be getting on his nerves. When I asked him about it, he just said, "No. But, just stay out of my way. I know what it's like to be out there on the cold days and I don't blame you at all."

Bud's condition wasn't getting any better, and he didn't come out of the house much. Missus Abercrombie had left to spend the winter in Florida, but assured us she would be back in April to help out. Sally came out on the better days, but spent a lot of time taking care of Bud. She did come every time we had work to do horseback, regardless of how cold it was. We had enough riding to do that her grulla and Bud's big paint were kept in good shape. Bud had given his big paint to Sally the year before as a wedding present.

My horse, Roman, was staying in good shape as was Drygulch, a company horse I had more or less appropriated as my own. We'd kept back some coming three-year-olds, or were they coming four-year-olds? I was starting to get confused. Dwight had been riding them and they were coming along good. Sally and I had ridden them quite a bit during the previous winter and summer.

In November, Pat, Bud, and I went to a bull sale and bought enough bulls to replace the bulls we had sold last fall. The bulls were delivered the following week and we got them branded, and then turned them out with the other bulls. We had been gone three days and I was relieved to find out Dwight had taken good care of everything while we were gone.

Dwight had proved to be a good hand and all that remained with him was to see how he got along with the dudes. I thought he would get along fine. One day, he asked, "Just what's the plan for the upcoming year?"

"We'll feed these cattle all winter," I said. "If the weather gets bad enough, we'll have to feed the broodmare band and the saddle horses. The replacement heifers we bred last year are scheduled to start calvin' in February, about thirty days before the regular cow herd. We'll calve them out in the feedlot. Course we'll have to check them at least twice a day. About January first, we'll start feedin' in the evening so the calves will come during the day, or at least later in the morning. We'll just take care of the cattle until the dudes start arrivin'. I think they'll start gettin' here about the middle of May, a little earlier than previous years. I'll have to check with Sally to see just what's happening.

"About the first of June, we'll start breeding our replacement heifers. We might be kinda busy with the replacements an' the dudes goin' on at the same time, but we'll manage. That's the overall plan, but it's subject to change on a daily basis."

Before Christmas, my folks called and invited Sally and me to come for a week and spend the holidays with them. I would have liked to have gone, but thought there was too much responsibility at the ranch to leave and Sally was very concerned about Bud's condition.

Sally and I did take a day to go to town and do some Christmas shopping. It was Sally's deal, she knew what to get everybody, and made her selections carefully. All I did was drive and pay for the purchases.

"We'll wrap these gifts for your family at the ranch, then come back to town and mail them," said Sally. "I'll need to bring Daddy in to the doctor's next week and I can get it done then."

It sounded to me like I wouldn't have to come to town, and I was relieved to know that. I like being at the ranch better than being in town.

We were making good progress halter breaking the colts. The more we handled them, the better they became. We also had the coming yearlings, from the year before, and the more we handled them, the better they became. We spent a lot of time teaching them how to load into a trailer. We'd neglected that in the past and had some problems after our first horse sale.

Pat, Dwight, and myself got kicked occasionally and the colts that kicked received more attention, just to get them used to being handled on a regular basis. I wouldn't let Sally handle any of the colts that were prone to kick; I couldn't have my wife getting hurt. The process wasn't really work, but it was time consuming and it gave us something to do. We could do it in the barn and we were out of the wind when it did blow. I was grateful for that; I didn't like a cold wind on a cold day.

Occasionally, Bud would come to the barn in the golf cart.

The cart tended to spook the colts, but we thought it would be good for them in furthering their education. They soon became used to it. Bud could hardly get out of the cart and getting the cart close to the colts so he could handle them only helped gentle them down.

"It's a good thing we ain't got much snow this year," said Pat. "If we had a lot of snow, you'd get that thing stuck!"

"I'm thinking I need a four-wheel drive outfit if we get a lot of snow," said Bud. "I don't know what I'll do."

"You can get a four-wheeler," said Dwight.

"What's that?"

"It's an outfit made for having fun. It's smaller than a truck; it will fit into the bed of a pickup. It's got four-wheel drive and it might be fairly useful for you. It's a gas-operated thing, and it should be more reliable that that battery-operated golf cart. I saw an advertisement for one in a hunting magazine. I'll get it for you and show it to you."

"I'd like to see it," said Bud. "I've never even heard of one before."

Bud spent a lot of time that night looking at the ads for the four-wheelers and was on the phone asking the manufacturers for information about them. He also asked for where their retail sales outlets were as we weren't aware of any in town.

Bud was anxious to see the advertisements when they came, and there were a lot of them. He spent a lot of time looking at the ads and on the phone talking to the dealers. His main concern was, could they be used with hand controls?

A lot of the dealers didn't know and a few offered to equip a vehicle with them and see. Bud set up appointments with the dealers that did it and made arrangements to go and have a test drive. He was very serious about the situation, although my first thoughts were that he was just looking to have a little fun.

A week before Christmas, Bud and Sally went to town. When

they returned, they announced that a new four-wheeler would be arriving in a few days. "That's going to be my new form of transportation," said Bud. "It should work better than the golf cart, although it worked pretty good. I should be able to go about anywheres Ol' Paint carried me. If I can't make it anywheres, I guess I don't need to go there. It'll be my Christmas present to myself."

"You should have seen him in town," said Sally. "He looked just like a kid in a toy store. He had a lot of fun trying out everything. I was sure he was going to wreck it before he even bought it."

"Does he have adequate hand controls?" I asked. I was a little concerned as Bud tended to drive a little fast.

"Oh yes," said Sally. "One of the dealers had them on an outfit so he could go right to driving. He bought it after driving it for about an hour, hand controls and all. That dealer must have figured on a sale and he figured right. I haven't seen him have that much fun in a long time. He seems to be in better spirits already. He was becoming a little depressed."

"I noticed that," I said. "I thought it was a little cabin fever."

"He should be over it now," said Sally. "But I'm still really concerned about him."

"His spirits should pick up as we get closer to spring," I said. I really didn't know what to do. Bud had always been active with the horses, cattle, and dudes and now he was reduced to riding a four-wheeler around. I did my best to keep him informed of what was going on around the ranch, but sometimes I thought it just depressed him more.

The day before Christmas, the four-wheeler arrived. Bud was really pleased and it took him a while before he volunteered to let anyone else try it out. Everybody got a chance to take it for a spin after getting instructions from the salesperson that delivered it. I really wasn't too interested in driving it, but Bud insisted.

"You might need to use it in an emergency," he said.

I took it for a spin and almost tipped it over, much to the amusement of everyone watching. It had more power than I thought. Dwight had driven one before and got along well with it. Pat was a little leery of it and almost tipped it over also. Sally was the most cautious.

"This is not a toy," she said, as she slowly drove it around the yard.

After everyone had a spin on the four-wheeler, Bud said, "You folks can use this in an emergency. Make sure you put it back where you got it from so you don't leave me afoot!"

An Extra Mouth to Feed

Christmas came and it was just another day. We got the chores done and relaxed in the lodge. New Years Day arrived and we started feeding the cattle in the afternoon. Sally, Pat, Dwight, and I rode out and checked the broodmare bunch.

"They look to be doing good," said Pat.

"I count an extra horse in there," I said. "How many do you count?"

"I get an extra one, too," said Sally.

"We better ride through 'em and see what's happenin', I said.

The mares wanted to run as we approached them and it was difficult to get a good look at all of them. Pat hollered, "Let's take 'em to the corrals an' get a good look at 'em! You two take the lead, Dwight an' I will bring up the rear."

Sally and I got ahead of them and led them toward the corrals. We did manage to slow them down a little. As we approached the corrals, I made a dash for the gate and swung it open and tried to get a count on the horses coming through.

"Yep," I said, "there's an extra horse there. I don't see any brands on him."

"Looks like he's about two years old," said Pat. "Probably one of them wild horses off the desert."

Sally said, "For your information, gentlemen, he's not a he. He's a she!"

"You're right Sally. It's a good thing we brought you along. We could have made a terrible mistake," said Pat, grinning.

"What are you going to do with her?" That was probably the first wild horse Dwight had ever seen. "She's not a bad looking horse."

"She's kinda undersized," said Pat. "I'll get a rope on her an' we'll separate her an' take the broodmares back. Bud will probably take her to the sale next week."

Pat roped the filly and dragged her, fighting, into another corral. We got Pat's rope off the filly and threw her some hay. Then we opened the gate and Sally and I led the broodmares back to their range. Pat and Dwight followed.

On the way back, Dwight said, "That's not a bad looking filly. I'd like to own her. Do you think Bud will let me keep her here?"

"You'll have to talk to Bud about that," I said.

"You know I could break her and use her here on the ranch. She could pay her own way!"

"That would be up to Bud," I said, hoping to end the conversation. I sure didn't want to firm up on this and then have Bud reverse the decision. "You need to talk to him about that."

Later that night, Bud made the decision to let Dwight keep the mustang.

The next day, Dwight started breaking the mustang. Pat and I were there to give him a hand, if he wanted it, but he seemed unwilling to heed our advice. Bud came down in the four-wheeler to watch.

Dwight had gotten a rope on the filly, but that was about all. He was on foot in the corral trying to gentle the horse down, but the horse wouldn't let him get anywhere close to her. Bud watched the proceedings and asked, "Just how many horses have you broke, Dwight?" Bud had a grin on his face when he asked the question.

Pat and I had been watching, holding back our laughter.

"This will be my first one," he said, gasping for air. "But I've read a lot about it." He appeared to be fighting a losing battle.

"You let Honey and Pat help you. Between them, they've probably broke more horses than you've ever rode. Honey here broke those paint horses you've been riding and there's nothing wrong with them. There's a big difference between reading about breaking a horse and actually doing it."

"Maybe I could use a hand," said Dwight. "I don't seem to be making much progress here."

"We'll help you, but only if you want us to," I said.

"Sure," said Dwight.

Pat rode his horse into the corral. I went in on foot, grabbed the dragging lariat rope on the filly and handed it to Pat.

"I'll get a hackamore," I said. "And some hobbles."

Pat had the filly snubbed up good and I got the hackamore on the horse. While she was standing there, I hobbled her front feet, but not without some problems. This was probably the first time she had been around people and naturally she was scared. Pat took his lariat rope off and we turned the filly loose.

"If she's got any smarts about her," said Pat, "it won't take her long to figure out she can't move well with the hobbles. Let's just leave her alone an' let her figure it out."

We left the filly to improve her education and did our chores. I noticed Dwight was continually looking toward the round pen as we did our work. I wondered if this mustang might be a distraction rather than asset.

At noon, we took the hobbles off the filly. "She's had enough education for today," I said. "We'll do the same thing tomorrow and add a little to her education."

After supper, I noticed Dwight down at the corral, trying to get close to his filly. He was bound and determined to make something out of his mustang.

"Time an' patience, Dwight, time an' patience," I said as I walked to the barn.

I left them alone and plugged in the two-way radios that I had forgotten to plug in.

If he keeps after it, he can make a horse out of her, I thought, when I went back to the lodge.

After a few days, Dwight could approach his filly. We continued with the hobbling lessons and started teaching the filly how to lead. It wasn't long before Dwight had the filly following him around the corral like a puppy. He was quite proud of his accomplishment. He started picking up her feet, just as we had done with the weaner colts.

"Do everything to her that we did to the weaners," said Pat. "Just take your time, she's doin' good. You let us know when you want to get on an' start ridin' her. We'll be here to help you."

"I think she's about ready," said Dwight. "What do you think?"

"Anytime," said Pat.

"Let's do it now," said Dwight. "I'm ready!"

"Let's do it tomorrow," said Pat. "We'll all be ready then."

"Okay, but I'll be a little anxious until then. Do you think she'll buck?"

"We'll do everything we can to keep her from buckin'," said Pat. "I don't think she'll buck hard, if she does buck. She's kinda small. But she might be pretty quick."

That night after supper, Pat and I were visiting. Dwight had gone down to the corral to visit with his filly.

I asked Pat, "Why did you put Dwight off about gettin' on his filly? We could have done it today."

Pat smiled. "I just wanted him to stew a little. He's quite excited about that little filly. I thought it might be fun. Besides, I thought it might be a good idea to long line her some. There's still a lot of fight in her. We'll see how it goes tomorrow."

The following day, Dwight was ready to get on his filly.

"Maybe we ought to long line her some before we get started," said Pat.

"I've been doing that every night after work," said Dwight.

"Show us," replied Pat.

Dwight caught the filly and proceeded to move her at a trot in a circle around him. When he'd flip the mecate and say "Whoa," the filly would stop. Then he'd trot her around in the opposite direction and repeat the exercise.

"It looks like you've done some good work with her," said Pat.

"Yes," I added, "I thought you were just down here every night just pettin' her. You've done good so far."

Dwight was pleased at Pat's comment and mine. "I think we're ready to get on her and ride her for the first time."

"I'll get my horse an' we'll get started," said Pat.

"I better saddle up, too," I said. "You might need some extra help."

Pat rode his saddled horse into the corral and I followed. Dwight handed the mecate on the filly to Pat and Pat snubbed her up close.

"Make sure your cinch is tight," Pat reminded Dwight. "Sometimes it's easy to forget the little things during the excitement!"

Dwight checked the cinch. "Are you ready?"

Pat nodded his head and Dwight put a foot and swung into the saddle easily. The filly jumped, but couldn't move much, Pat had her snubbed pretty tight.

"Just sit there for a spell," said Pat. "Rock back an' forth in the saddle some. This is all new to her an' we'll give her a good chance to get used to it. Don't rush her none."

Dwight did as instructed and the filly, although she was a little edgy, took it fairly calmly.

"Now we'll move out a little," said Pat. "I'll give her some slack an' you touch her with your heels."

Dwight did as he was told and the filly was reluctant to move. I rode up behind her.

"Hold on," I said as I flipped the end of my lariat rope on her rump.

When the filly felt the rope on her rump, she jumped forward. The jump loosened Dwight a little and he started leaning to the right a little. I moved my horse up beside the filly and pushed Dwight back square in the saddle. Pat had moved his horse forward and the filly reluctantly followed.

"Keep her moving," said Pat. "I'll play out a little line an' we'll have her goin'. She'll soon get the idea."

Sally and Bud had come to the corral in the four-wheeler to watch. "She doesn't want to move easy," said Bud. "Keep after her, she's just learning!"

Pat kept leading the filly in the round corral. I followed, ready to use my lariat rope on the filly if needed. The little horse followed Pat a little more willingly.

"Give her a little more encouragement," said Pat. "We'll trot her out. She still doesn't know what's happenin'."

Dwight spurred the filly and she jumped out. Pat still had her pretty close and she couldn't do much, but she did jump once and then started to trot. We trotted around the corral to the left, then changed directions and went around to the right. After about half an hour, Pat said, "That's enough for today! Turn her loose an' let her think about it. We'll do the same thing tomorrow."

I could see Dwight was disappointed. I think he wanted to break the horse in one day and start using her on the ranch. But he did as he was told and we started our chores for the day.

Dwight was full of questions about how his filly acted on

the first ride and what we thought of her. It was plain that he was excited about breaking his first horse. I soon tired of the questions and said, "Let's see how she acts tomorrow. After thinkin' about it over night, she might decide she doesn't want to be a saddle horse and put up a pretty good fight."

This comment only led to more questions from Dwight. "Then what will we do? And how will we do it?"

"We'll just have to see," I said, hoping to end the conversation. "Let's get this hay loaded an' finish our chores."

The next day we resumed the filly's training. She didn't resist as much and our session went fairly well.

"She appears to be a slow learner," said Pat. "We'll have to do quite a bit of this to keep her goin'. It'll take some time."

Dwight appeared concerned over Pat's comment. "Do you think she'll ever get it?"

"Yes, she'll get it," said Pat. "Sometimes these slow learners remember what they learn better than the fast ones. Right, Honey?"

"You're only sayin' that because you've had some slow learners in your personal horses," I said. I was remembering some colts of Pat's that I'd started that were slow learners.

"But they turned out to be good horses!"

"True," I said. "But it took a whole lot of work to make 'em that way. I really think they turned out to be good horses because of the horse trainer, rather than some inherited ability they had! I know I had to do a lot of work with them."

I was having some fun with Pat while slyly bragging up my own horse training skills.

Pat laughed. "I don't know about that. The horse has to have some aptitude to start with!"

"True," I said, "but it takes a good horse trainer with a lot of skill to bring it out with some horses. I had to work doubly hard with your horses to get them to do anythin'! The fact that they became anythin' at all is only a testament to the trainer's skills an' knowledge!"

I was laying it on pretty thick. Pat was still laughing, enjoying this verbal exchange. I wasn't going to let him get the best of me, but we were both having a lot of fun. Dwight watched this exchange not knowing what was really happening.

We worked the filly for about half an hour then turned her loose and did our chores. Our routine became pretty much the same every day; we'd feed the replacement heifers in the morning, Dwight would ride his filly for half an hour or so, we'd mess with the weaner colts and yearlings, then feed the cows toward evening. When we had some slack time, we'd tend to other chores, like mending broken equipment. We did manage to stay busy.

After a few days, Dwight got on his filly without the horse being snubbed up. Pat still had the mecate, just in case the filly tried to do something. So far, Dwight had only ridden the horse in the round pen, but Pat had given the filly plenty of slack on the mecate. Eventually, Pat wasn't keeping the mecate at all. Dwight was riding the filly all on his own.

Dwight asked, "Do you think we can go outside the pen? This is getting pretty boring in here."

"I thought you'd never ask," said Pat. "You're in charge of this little project; you're supposed to tell us what you want when you're ready. Ain't that right, Honey?"

"Absolutely," I answered. "I been pretty bored myself in this round pen."

"But," said Dwight, "she's a slow learner. I didn't want to rush her too much. Let's go outside!"

I opened the gate from horseback and led the way out. "Follow me," I told Dwight, and started out at a walk.

The filly followed my horse, not knowing what to expect.

Pat followed the filly and I couldn't tell if Dwight was riding the horse or Pat was driving the horse.

After we'd went about a hundred yards or so, I said, "Let's hurry this up a little," and moved my horse into a trot. I was watching Dwight and the filly. They moved easily into a trot.

We were moving out at a trot when suddenly Dwight and the filly passed me at a run! Dwight was having a runaway! The filly was trying to buck a little as she ran.

I knew it was futile to try and catch them; the filly would think it was a horse race and just run faster.

"Get her goin' in a circle," I yelled. "An' keep her goin' in a circle! She'll soon tire an' slow down. When she wants to slow down, you keep her goin'. Teach her that she's supposed to do what you want her to do!"

I was following at a trot when Pat rode up beside me. He had a real big grin on his face and it was hard for him to keep from laughing out loud.

"I guess I shouldn't have encouraged the horse," he said, as he tried to hold back his laughter. "Dwight might have more than he can handle there!"

I started to laugh, I couldn't help it. "You're responsible for this?"

"Sort of," answered Pat. "The filly was laggin' a little an' Dwight asked me to sorta help her. Maybe I gave her too much help."

We stopped our horses to watch. Dwight was all over the saddle, but he hadn't been thrown off. He was slowly getting the filly to circle. As he loped back toward us, the filly was starting to tire.

"Keep her moving," I said. "Get her tired an' she won't be so inclined to do that again!"

Dwight made a circle around us and I said, "That's good. Give her a rest now."

Dwight stopped the horse and she was content to stand.

"Looks like she might have woke up," said Pat. "It appears that she might have some spunk to her."

"That surprised me," said Dwight. "But it was fun. Do you think she'll amount to anything?"

"We'll have to see," I said. "It appears she can move out when she wants to." I winked at Pat and he stifled a laugh.

"I think she's had enough for today," said Pat. "Maybe too much. Let's head back."

Toward the end of January, I started riding through the first calf heifers twice a day, looking for early calvers. Most of the time Sally would accompany me, just to get some riding time. She would either ride the big paint or her grulla. Dwight would come along, riding his filly.

"You've got the filly started good, Dwight," I told him one day, "but you need to be ridin' some of these other horses. You don't want to be ridin' that filly into the ground. A little each day is better than a whole lot all at once."

I could tell Dwight liked riding the filly, but I thought he might be overdoing it a little.

In February, the first calvers started to calve. We had to pull a few calves and tried to stay on top of things. We were real busy the first part of February; the heifers were calving on a regular basis. We lost a couple of calves and Bud told me to go to the sale and buy a couple of day old calves to graft onto the heifers.

"Take Sally with you, I think she's getting a little cabin fever here. The change will do her some good."

Sally and I went to town and the brief change did do her some good. While we were in town, I got a hold of the manager of the dairy and asked him about buying the calves directly from him. If we could do that, it would save having to milk the heifer out twice a day until sale day.

The manager of the dairy agreed and gave me his phone

number. "Call when you need a calf. If we've got one, come and get him. That might save me some time having to haul them to the sale."

I told Bud what I'd done and he said, "That's a good idea. Why didn't I think of it?"

"It might save us some time an' money," I said. "We'll see."

Wild Times

The calving was going well. We'd lost a couple of calves, but had managed to graft some calves on the heifers. Dwight was a big help and he was riding his filly in a regular rotation with the two paint horses. The filly was coming along; riding in the muddy pens was helping her to build some muscle and stamina.

It was easy riding, just walking looking for heifers that were ready to calve and looking for sick heifers in the weaner pens. The mud did make it a little tough on the horses, but it helped them stay in shape.

Toward the end of February we started riding through the main cow herd in the mornings looking for cows that were ready to calve. We could check them in the afternoon when we fed. Pat had been riding through the cows in the morning while Dwight and I rode through the heifers. As the number of first calvers dwindled, we had more time to assist Pat.

I think Dwight really enjoyed riding through the cows more than riding through the heifers. He could move his horse out faster and had more room. His filly hadn't tried to run off with him since the first day he rode her out of the round pen.

One day while Pat, Dwight, and I were checking the cows, we noticed a cow limping in the pasture. Sally didn't come along as she wasn't feeling well. I thought she had a touch of the flu.

"We better rope her an' see what's wrong," I said, taking down my rope.

Dwight already had his rope down and had a loop built. He headed toward the cow and started to swing his rope. His filly got nervous, and started to run off. Dwight threw his loop at the cow, and his filly, surprised, ducked away and started to buck.

Surprisingly enough, Dwight's loop was true and he caught the cow. He managed to take his dallies while his horse was bucking. That might have proven to be a mistake, because when the cow hit the end of the rope, the filly was in mid air.

The cow was pretty big and managed to pull the filly over backward. Dwight jumped clear before the horse landed on him. He still had the end of his rope dallied to the saddle horn and the cow caught. The cow was still on her feet, but couldn't move. The filly, lying on the ground acted like dead weight and the cow could only move as far as the rope, dallied to the saddle horn, would allow her to.

The filly was trying to get up, but the rope attached to the cow kept her on the ground.

I couldn't help but laugh. Dwight had caught the cow, but was afoot and it appeared like the cow had caught the horse! I really didn't know who had caught who!

Pat was laughing so hard he could hardly stay in the saddle, much less make a loop with his rope to help out. I managed to make a loop but couldn't control my own laughter.

The cow was starting to get mad and charged Dwight, still holding onto the end of his rope. The cow had all the slack in the rope between her and the filly to work with. Dwight didn't have enough room to get out of the way of the cow and still hold onto the rope.

The whole scene was hilarious! The horse was on the ground, the cow was chasing Dwight and Dwight still had a hold of the end of his rope. Nobody seemed to know who was caught!

The cow was gaining ground on Dwight. The situation was becoming serious and Pat regained his composure enough to build a loop and rope the cow. But not before the cow hit Dwight, sending him into the air. He landed about ten feet away.

Pat hollered, "Honey! Quit you're gigglin' an' help hold this cow. We come out here to doctor this cow, remember?"

I stopped laughing long enough to rope the cow's hind feet and Pat and I stretched her out.

"Dwight," I said, "there's some penicillin an' a syringe in my saddle bag. Get 'em an' give her a shot. The cure may have been worse than the illness for this old gal. I think it's just a touch of foot rot."

Dwight gave the cow a shot.

"Now, get your horse, take off the head ropes an' get out of the way. I'll keep her stretched out until you're on your horse, then turn her loose. Hurry though, she might have other plans. I think she took a likin' to you an' might want to become better acquainted."

Dwight did as he was told. Pat couldn't stop laughing as he coiled his rope. When I loosened the slack in my rope, the cow got up and headed toward Dwight an' the filly. They quickly got out of the way and the cow ran off.

"I think that cow still likes you," I said, laughing.

"Just who had caught who? I was wonderin'," said Pat.

Undaunted, Dwight just said, "We got the job done, didn't we?"

"Yes," said Pat. "But we could have been a little more professional about it. It started to look like a circus out there!"

"Maybe so," replied Dwight. "But I'll bet that cow has second thoughts about getting foot rot again!"

I just laughed. It looked like Dwight would fit in, all the way around.

"I can't wait to tell Sally, Bud, an' the cook about this," I said. "I'll bet Sally will regret missin' this little episode."

"You'll probably embellish it and blow it all out of proportion," said Dwight.

"I don't think so," said Pat. "It don't need no embellishin' as it stands. There's no way it could stand any improvement."

We finished checking the cows and rode back to the ranch. Pat chuckled and even broke out into laughter occasionally on the way home.

He kept saying, "I can't wait to tell everyone. It's a good story to tell the dudes! They'll really enjoy it an' you might even become famous!"

Dwight was fairly easy going and he even started to laugh as Pat retold the story, over and over.

"You should have seen the look on your face," said Pat. "Were you actually surprised that you caught the cow? An' you should have seen the look on the horse's face. She didn't know what was happenin'. The cow was also surprised! I think Honey an' me was also surprised! And did you see how far that cow tossed you? This is the best event that's happened here for a few years."

"Yeah," said Dwight. "I'll probably have a bruise."

"If you do," said Pat, "you can use a pillow when we ride tomorrow. Ask Sally if you can use one from the guest's rooms. We won't need them for a while."

Pat was relentless in his teasing of Dwight, and there wasn't anything Dwight could do about it—it was all true.

I did take Dwight aside and said, "You might want to start throwin' a rope off that filly just to get her used to the action an' the swingin' of the rope. You don't have to catch anything, just throw it. That will help as much as anything. Then, start ropin' smaller stuff, calves. Work into it easy. You asked that little filly to do more than what she could do today. You might start draggin' a few things around, like some hay bales. That will help. But, that's part of her education.

"You an' that filly have been through a lot today, better give her the day off tomorrow."

Dwight asked, "Me too?"

"No," I said. "You'll have to work."

I noticed as Dwight rode, he'd take his rope down and start swinging it just to get the filly used to it. He was bound and determined to make a good horse out of her.

More Surprises

Supper that night was humorous to say the least. Pat enjoyed telling the story of Dwight's roping the cow and everyone had a good laugh over it. Bud got to laughing so hard that he could hardly eat.

He asked, "Just who had caught who?"

"We ain't got that figured out yet," said Pat. "It might be the mystery of the year!"

When we finished supper, Bud said, "I'm going to have Sally take me to town tomorrow. Do you guys need anything?"

"I might could use some horse liniment," said Dwight.

"There's plenty down in the barn," said Bud. "Use it. Save your money."

"I can't think of anything I need," I said.

"I know what you need," said Sally. "I'll get it for you. And I'll get the same things for you, Pat."

Pat gave her a surprised look. "I was just goin' to say some razor blades an' shavin' cream."

"Like I said," said Sally, "I'll get the same things for you!"

Pat grinned. "That's almost like bein' married!"

I didn't know what Bud was going to town for, but his trips were becoming more frequent. I suspected it had something to do with his worsening condition. I didn't want to bring it up to him as I knew he didn't like to talk about it. I knew he'd tell us when he was ready.

Bud and Sally returned later that day with a motorized wheelchair on a rack affixed to the rear of the company car. He also had a regular wheelchair in the back seat of the car.

"I guess it's coming to this," he said, as Sally unloaded the motorized wheelchair.

I took the wheelchair from the back seat.

"Put that on the four-wheeler, on the backseat," said Bud. "I'll be able to get around wherever I am. I don't know what I'll do when I can't handle this."

"Keep your spirits up Bud," I said. "We'll figure somethin' out."

I got a couple of sacks from Sally.

"One is for you and one is for Pat. They're both the same; shaving stuff. Give one to Pat then come to the lodge, I need to talk to you."

Sally sounded pretty serious. I gave a sack to Pat and went back to the lodge, wondering what Sally was so serious about. I wondered if she had something besides the flu, she had mentioned something about going to the doctor's.

I went to the lodge and Sally was waiting in the dining room. "Come with me," she said, taking my hand and leading me to our living quarters. In our quarters, she closed the door, put her arms around me and kissed me passionately. I was totally surprised.

"I love you very, very, very much, Honey," she said.

I wondered what was happening and just stood there waiting for her to tell me. I didn't know if it was good news or bad news, or if it concerned Bud or her or me. I felt kinda foolish standing there without having anything to say.

"Aren't you going to ask me what's happening?"

"Well … ah … I sorta thought you'd get around to it … eventually. What is happening? I really don't know what to say."

"I went to the doctor's. I'm pregnant!"

I really didn't know what to say now! I stammered and stuttered, "How? Ah … when? I mean … you mean you don't have the flu?"

"No," said Sally, "I don't have the flu. And you know how, Silly. When? I'm due in November. I'm so happy. I didn't even tell Daddy on the way home. I wanted you to be the first to know! You can tell everyone at supper!"

Sally was excited! I hadn't given much thought to becoming a father and I was sorta stunned. "I better sit down, before I fall down," I said.

"Yes," said Sally. "You better relax. I didn't think it would be such a shock to you!" Sally could see that I was clearly affected.

"Aren't you happy?"

"Well … ah … yes. I'm just sorta shocked." I said.

"After you tell everyone here, I'll call your folks and tell them the news. You're mother will be so happy! She told me she was looking forward to being a grandmother."

"You mean you have discussed this with my mother?"

"Well, of course. We thought three would be a good number," said Sally.

"Three! All at once?" I was still a little shocked.

"No, no. Spread out over a few years, Silly."

I didn't know what to think or do. How was a new father to be supposed to act? I had no idea. I rested, sitting down and gave the matter some thought. Slowly, I was becoming used to the idea of becoming a father, but it was taking some time.

"I suppose, Darlin'," I said, "we're committed now! I just don't know what to do."

"You don't have to do anything, Honey. I'll do it all."

"Are you sure? There must be something I can do. I don't want to feel like I've been left out of this deal!"

"Oh," said Sally, "you haven't been! No, you haven't been! You've been very instrumental in the whole thing!" Sally was grinning that mischievous grin she had.

"If you say so," I said.

"Now," she said, "you better go get your chores done. And don't tell anyone until after supper!"

"Yes, ma'am," I said. I got up to leave, but not before giving Sally a kiss and a big hug.

The chores went by fairly easily that night, and I didn't really pay much attention to what I was doing.

Pat noticed this and said, "You better drive while we feed. You're mind isn't on your job. Is everything all right with Bud and Sally?"

"Everything's all right," I assured Pat. "I've just got some other things on my mind."

I wondered how Sally kept from telling her dad on the way home. I thought she must be made of steel, although I knew different.

After supper, I started to make our announcement. Pat and Dwight had already got up and were taking their dishes to the sink.

"When you put them away," I said, "Come back an' sit down. I have an announcement to make."

I waited until Pat and Dwight returned to the table. Trying to be very serious, I said, "There's goin' to be some changes around here, an' they're goin' to start right now."

Pat and Bud looked surprised. Dwight looked bewildered and a little scared.

"It has come to my attention recently, and I need to apologize to you guys for it because it will mean the loss in the future of one of our best hands, that my wife, Sally, has become pregnant. I don't know when this happened, although I have been assured I was present when it happened ..."

"Pregnant!" Bud interrupted. "You mean I'm going to become a grandfather? Congratulations Honey! And to you too, Daughter! And to me, too! A grandfather! I can't believe it!"

I saw Sally giggling. She was pleased.

Bud wheeled himself around to hug Sally. Pat came over, shook my hand and congratulated me. Dwight did the same thing, following Pat's lead. Bud wheeled himself around and shook my hand vigorously.

"Congratulations, my boy, congratulations! Just think, a grandfather!"

I asked him, "Are you congratulatin' me or you?"

"Both of us, Honey, both of us!"

It was obvious Bud was pleased.

The cook came over and congratulated me, then gave Sally a big hug. "I'll have to brush up on my baby recipes," he said. "It's been awhile since I've had to fix formulas."

Sally smiled. She was radiant. "We need to call Honey's parents. We haven't told everybody yet. We wanted you to be the first."

She left and went to the phone. It was hard for me to get away, accepting everyone's congratulations.

Sally called my folks, told them the news, and then called me to the phone. I accepted their congratulations, then inquired as to how things were on their ranch. We visited for a while and I handed the phone back to Sally.

She visited with my mother for a spell, then they concluded their conversation. Sally then called Missus Abercrombie, and told her.

Missus Abercrombie said, "I'll make arrangements to come out there immediately. You'll need some help."

Sally tried to assure her that it wasn't necessary, but Missus Abercrombie wouldn't take no for an answer.

Missus Abercrombie told Sally she'd get a flight on the first available plane. "Don't worry about making up my room, I can do that. I'll call later to let you know what flight I'll be on and what day I'll be there. Just have someone at the airport to pick me up."

Bud called Fred and told him the news and told him to tell Rod. Rod didn't have a phone.

The news was out.

Missus Abercrombie arrived three days later and Sally went to town to pick her up. I was at the lodge when they arrived from town, and took her bags to her room. She didn't have much, she'd left quite a bit at the ranch when she left last fall.

I accepted her congratulations and thought I'd have a little fun with her.

"Ain't it grand that Bud built that new calvin' shed awhile back? An' you gave us an electric heater. We won't even have to leave the ranch when the baby comes. We can handle it right here. Bud must have known somethin' like this would happen. He's got a lot of foresight."

"The baby will be born in a hospital," said Missus Abercrombie, very business like, "and it will be delivered by a doctor, not a cowboy."

I could see my humor was not being accepted very well and stopped that line of joking. "Yes, ma'am."

"I've been thinking," said Sally. "I think we need to start a Wilson Ranch newsletter and send it out once a month to our former guests and family members. We could keep them informed of what's happening on the ranch and keep the Wilson Ranch name in front of them more often. It might mean more reservations in the future and we could advertise our calf sales and horse sales. We've had quite a bit of correspondence from previous guests asking how things are at the ranch. We could also announce things like this. The phone would become too expensive. Yes, I think I'll do it."

She didn't wait for anyone's approval, as far as she was concerned, it was a done deal. She just needed to do it, and she started that night.

The next few days were spent in serious contemplation for me. The thought of being a father was new to me. I wasn't sure how I would or should act.

We lost another calf and I called the dairy to see if they had one available. They had one, he'd been born three days ago and I could buy him if I wanted him. I said I wanted him and that I'd be there sometime after noon.

I asked Sally, "Do you want to go for a ride?"

"Sure. Where are you going?"

"We lost a calf this morning. I called the dairy, they've got one an' we can buy him if we want. I'm goin' right now to get him."

"I'll go with you," she said.

We got my truck and a tarp. I figured I'd rig up a windbreak to help protect the calf from the wind traveling down the road. I told Pat where we were headed and what time we expected to be back.

"Dwight an' me will take care of the chores. We'll have the heifer ready to accept the calf when you get back."

"Good," I said. "We'll try to get back early."

We left. It occurred to me that Sally and I hadn't had a chance to talk much since the announcement of her pregnancy. I think it occurred to Sally also.

"What do you think of it?"

"What?" I was pretty sure I knew what she was talking about, but wanted to make sure.

"The baby," she said. "What else is there?"

"It's kinda scary," I said. "I'm not sure how to act or what to do."

"You just keep doing what you're doing. You're doing okay."

"Yea, but bein' a father is new to me. I never been one before!"

"I've never been a mother before," said Sally. "But I think it's kinda exciting. I'm looking forward to it."

"It is kinda exciting," I conceded. "But it is also kinda scary."

Sally slid over as close as she could get to me. "When you get scared, you just tell me. I'll help you through it. We're partners, remember?"

"You've got a deal," I said.

We picked up the calf, got something to eat in town and headed back to the ranch. When we got there, Pat was at the calving sheds. He was ready, just like he said he'd be.

After a few days we had successfully grafted the calf onto the heifer.

The newness of Sally's pregnancy began to wear off. Although I was aware of it, I wasn't constantly thinking of it as I had been a few days earlier. I was returning to some degree of normalcy.

I went to Bud one day and said, "I been thinkin'."

"Oh really! What else is new?" Bud interrupted. He was being sarcastic with me, looking to have a little fun. His spirits had improved considerably since the announcement of Sally's pregnancy.

"I would like to go to another bull sale an' buy a Black Angus bull to use as a cleanup bull on our replacement heifers. We had a pretty fair conception rate on them, something like eighty-five percent, if I remember right. If we had a cleanup bull, we might get better than that. And those Angus bulls are supposed to throw small calves."

"Do you think it would be worthwhile?" Bud asked.

"I think it's worth a try. We could keep the replacements separate for a few more weeks with the bull, and then pull him out. We won't know if it works until we preg check in the fall. We could either keep the bull separate, or sell him as soon as his job's done."

"Let's give it a try," said Bud. "As you know, I'm fairly open to trying new ideas. Some of them haven't paid off, but this one shows promise. Where do you want to go to a sale at?"

I showed him some sale flyers I'd been looking at. "Any one of these should fill the bill. There are some pretty nice lookin' bulls for sale. We could buy one of the two-year-olds an' try him out."

"I'd like to go with you when you go," he said.

"Sure. I figured I'd take Sally. It might be a three-day trip, maybe four, depending on what sale we go to. I'd like to go before the dudes start arriving."

"Just plan on it," said Bud. "Oh, by the way, we'll have to start thinking about advertising for hired help. I'll probably go to the college again and interview. Do you want to go?"

"Not really," I said. "I don't really feel comfortable in town."

"Well then, do you mind if I take Sally? She's been a great help to me in these kinds of matters."

"Of course not! She can go if she wants to, but I wouldn't force her," I said. "Course, she may not want to go, but she will. She has never shirked any duties with regards to the ranch. That's just one of the things I admire about her so much."

"I'll get with her and we'll make plans. I think we should start in April, get everyone hired and get them here as close to the middle of May as possible. You know, we're bringing dudes in a little earlier this year than we have in the past. We can plan our bull selling trip for the end of April or beginning of May. You figure out what sale coincides with those dates and let me know. I'll make room arrangements and handle everything."

I simply said "Okay." One thing about Bud, when he made up his mind to do something, he generally got it done. There wasn't much room for second thoughts.

Sally continued to ride with us as we checked the cattle. I wondered if it was good for her in her condition. She assured me it was all right. She said, "I checked with the doctor and he said as long as I had been riding and was used to it, it shouldn't hurt anything. He told me some of his horsewomen patients had ridden right up to their ninth month without any problems."

"That might be all right for them," I said, "but this is my kid. He's special an' we're goin' to make sure everythin' is as good as we can make it for him."

Sally asked, "How do you know it's going to be a boy?"

"What else could it be, a puppy?" I was going to have a little fun with Sally.

"It could be a girl."

I asked, "What do we want with a girl puppy? What would we do with it?"

"We'll just have to see what it is. And it won't be a puppy. Daddy doesn't want dogs around. We better start thinking about names."

"Okay, I guess we can eliminate Fido," I said. "You figure out what possibilities we have an' we'll decide when the time comes. I'm thinkin' I'll need to go to town with you when you go in for your checkups."

"That's not necessary," said Sally. "Daddy or Missus Abercrombie can go with me."

"Nope," I said. "I sorta think that's my job. Even though I don't much care for town, I'd better do my duties."

"Whatever you say," said Sally. "You're the boss."

"I'm not so sure about that," I said. "But somebody has to do it."

March had arrived and the winter was passing. The days

were getting longer. The first calf heifers were just about done calving and the main cow herd had started. Once again there was a lot of color among the calves of the first calvers. They were half Texas Longhorns.

While we were checking the cows one morning, Pat commented, "I sure like the idea of feedin' in the evenin' so as the calves are born towards mornin'. Your dad had a pretty good idea. It beats gettin' up around one or two in the middle of the night to check 'em. I've lost a lot of sleep over the years."

"It wasn't my dad's idea," I said. "He'd read it in a magazine somewhere an' tried it out. It seemed to work, so he stayed with it. It appears to be workin' here. We'll keep usin' it. You know, I'll have to be takin' Sally into town for her checkups. Can you an' Dwight handle everythin'?"

"I'll bet we can manage," said Pat. "Dwight's been provin' to be a pretty fair hand. You just do what you need to do an' don't worry about things while you're gone. We'll handle it."

I knew everything would be all right and appreciated Pat's reassurance.

The main cow herd was calving pretty regular and without much problem. Checking the cow herd became routine. When we'd get about fifty cows that had calves, we'd move them into a separate pasture. We'd keep these little herds of fifty or so into separate pastures. It was part of a pasture rotation program and it allowed us to brand every couple of weeks so all the guests could experience the branding. It was a unique program and toward the end of the summer, some of the calves would be pretty big. We'd team rope them, head and heel them to get them branded.

By the middle of March, we had all the first calvers calved out. I kept them all in a separate pasture so we could use the Angus bull I intended on buying as a cleanup bull. I hadn't decided which sale to go to; I'd have to be making up my mind fairly quickly. I studied the pictures in the sale catalogs carefully and decided upon a couple of prospects. The sale I decided on was about a day's drive away. That would mean a day to get there, a day at the sale, and a day back.

The bull sale I decided upon was going to take place toward the end of April. I checked with Bud to see if the dates would conflict with his college interview plans.

"I think it will work out good. Sally and I can go to the college, do our interviews, then meet you at the sale. Sally and I will be gone about a week and we can follow you back to the ranch with your new bull. You'll only be gone about three days. Does that sound right to you?"

"That's about the way I had it planned," I said. "You an' Sally can take the company car an' I'll take the two-ton truck."

"Good! I'll make room reservations at the proper places and we'll plan on it. You better write down the dates of the sale so I don't get things confused."

I gave Bud the sale dates and went out to feed the cows.

Away From the Ranch

March quickly passed and April came. With it came the proverbial April showers. We had plenty of room at the calving sheds and we moved the cows that hadn't calved to the calving sheds. I thought having the new calves under the sheds during the rains might help them get a better start on life.

Sally continued to ride with us as we checked the cattle and moved them into new pastures. I was concerned about this and when I took her to town for her checkup, I asked the doctor about it. He reassured me that it was fine, all the riding Sally had done had got her in shape. She could continue to ride without any adverse consequences. I left feeling better about Sally's riding.

Sally continued with her other chores, including making her first copy of the Wilson Ranch newsletter. She mailed it out the first of April. Much to my surprise, the newsletter contained a lot of information about the ranch history that I didn't know, and what was going on during the winter. Sally only gave a paragraph regarding her pregnancy and listed her due date as November. She concluded with the statement, "Both Honey and I are thrilled, although Honey is still a little bewildered."

The newsletter generated a lot of response from previous guests sending their congratulations. It also generated a few reservations for the upcoming summer. We also got a letter from

Jim, the guy that had been our head housekeeper for the last few years. He wanted to come back to work for us.

Bud noted the response to the newsletter and was very positive about it. "Why didn't I think of it? That's what we need around here, some new thinking! Make sure you hire Jim again, Sally, he's good help." He was pleased with the results.

"I've already hired Jim. He'll be here in the first part of May," said Sally. "I've also given him a raise, he deserves it."

"Good," said Bud. "Good!"

Sally also packed a bag for me to take to the bull sale, while packing her and Bud's bags. She was not slowing down.

Bud and Sally left to go to the college to interview prospective employees for the summer. We needed maids, a kitchen helper, and another wrangler or two. I wasn't sure how much we would be able to use Sally, and tried to impress upon Bud that we surely didn't want to come up short-handed.

They left, but only after making sure I would meet them at the hotel Bud had made reservations at. I assured them I would be there. "I'll be there, but don't have any idea what time. If I'm late, don't wait up for me. It all depends on what time I can get away from here. Just make sure you hire some good help an' get them here as early as possible. You know we have dudes … er, guests coming in the middle of May."

The next few days were pretty much routine, with the exception that I had to answer the phone in the evenings. A lot of the calls came from previous guests, offering their congratulations on the news of the pregnancy. I did make a few reservations for the upcoming summer. A few calls came regarding the help wanted ad Bud had put in the livestock papers. I set up some appointments to meet with these applicants when Bud and Sally returned.

Sally called each night, just to see how things were going. I told her what we had been doing with the cattle, and what I had been doing on the phone, with regard to reservations.

"Make sure you don't overbook us," cautioned Sally. "It looks like we're going to have a pretty full summer."

"I think we're all right," I said. "I'd suggest a big chart on the wall showin' what cabins an' rooms are available for what dates. It might make it a little easier to make reservations."

"Good idea," said Sally. "I'll start on it tonight when we've completed our interviews. I love you Honey. And I miss you."

"Me too," I said and hung up.

The day came for me to go to the bull sale. I didn't need to give Pat or the cook any instructions, they knew what to do. I got my suitcase and left for the sale.

At the hotel that night I met Sally and Bud. Sally was pleased to see me. That night, Sally showed me a rough sketch she'd made. She had each room or cabin listed down the left side of the paper. Across the top, she'd listed the dates by week. The chart went from the middle of May to the middle of October.

"Looks like we'll be extending our season," I said.

"I think we should," said Sally. "It's a ready source of income and the facility just sits idle when the rooms and cabins aren't being used."

"It will mean keepin' some extra help into the fall," I said.

"If we can keep the rooms or cabins fairly full, we can make money. What do you think of my chart? I'm going to have it printed up on a blackboard when we go through town."

"The chart is a good idea, but you need to make room on it so you can mark down if they've paid a deposit an' how much," I said.

"Good idea! You're really getting into the dude end of this ranch!"

I could tell Sally was pleased.

The next day we went to the bull sale early so we could look over all the prospects. Sally and Bud took the car and I took the truck.

I told Bud, "If we can get this done early, we can make it back to the ranch today." I didn't relish another night in town.

Bud's comment was simple, "Fat chance," he said.

We watched the bull sale and I bid on a few prospects, but without success. I had a price in mind and I didn't want to exceed it.

Bud watched. "You're going to have to raise your thinking a little. These bulls are selling a little higher than you thought."

"I don't want to spend too much money," I said.

"But," said Bud, "I wouldn't let these bulls get away for fifty bucks or less. We don't want to come away empty-handed and have to go to another sale."

Bud's advise was not wasted. I raised my thinking and after bidding on three bulls without success, I managed to buy one.

"That bull cost me more than I wanted to spend," I said.

Bud laughed. "That bull didn't cost you a thing! But he cost me plenty!"

I had to laugh. "Maybe I came out all right," I said.

It was too late to load the bull and try to get back to the ranch that day. I made arrangements to leave the bull there overnight on feed and water and to leave the truck there. We'd get an early start the next day.

That night at supper we discussed the new help Sally and Bud had hired.

"We've got three girls hired as maids," said Sally. "With Jim's help they should be all right. We've only got one wrangler hired. He's a little green, but seems willing to learn. We also hired a cook's helper for our cook. This guy wants to become a chef and I'm sure our cook can show him quite a few tricks. I think he said he was majoring in culinary arts or something like that."

"I've made arrangements to interview some prospective hands that answered our newspaper ad. They'll be showin' up after we get back," I said.

The next day we loaded the bull and started for the ranch. Sally and Bud drove together and I took the bull. I noticed that Sally and Bud pulled off as we went through town. Thinking something was wrong, I pulled over and went looking for them.

I found them in the hardware store looking at the ads for handymen.

"What's up?"

"We're just going to get our chart made up and we're looking for a handyman to do it," said Sally. "Is everything all right?"

"Yes," I said. "I thought you were havin' trouble an' came to see if I could help."

"You're so sweet," said Sally and she gave me a kiss. "But we can handle things here. Go to the ranch, we'll meet you there."

"Okay."

I drove on to the ranch and unloaded the bull at the calving sheds. Pat was waiting for me.

"I hope you don't mind," he said. "We lost a calf an' I took your truck to the dairy an' got a calf to graft onto the cow."

"No," I said, "I don't mind. That's why I leave the keys in the truck. How much did the calf cost?"

Pat told me and I said, "I'll send 'em a check."

"That won't be necessary," said Pat. "I paid for him, cash."

I reached for my wallet and reimbursed Pat. "What do you think of our new bull?"

"He's a different color than what we're used to here," said Pat.

"We're goin' to use him on our replacements as I'd told you." I'd run my idea past Pat before presenting it to Bud. "Maybe we can get a higher conception rate. We won't turn him in with the heifers until we're done artificially breedin'. We'll keep him with the heifers for about forty-five days. That should give him plenty of time to catch the heifers we might have missed."

We branded the bull and put him in a separate pen from the heifers. We'd decide on whether or not to keep him when we were done with the heifers. We might want to turn him out with the main cow herd after he'd finished his main job—covering the heifers that might be open.

We interviewed applicants for the wrangling positions the following week. We hired one guy right on the spot, a feller named Scott Murphy. He was the son of a neighboring rancher and had been raised on their ranch. Bud and Pat knew him fairly well and he was already familiar with a lot of the country.

The day after we hired Scott, we went out to bring in the broodmare bunch and brand the colts. We also needed to take photographs of each colt for registration purposes.

I was adamant about Sally not going, although she really wanted to. I put my foot down, by saying, "That's generally a pretty wild time. What if your horse should stumble and fall. You could injure not only yourself, but the baby also. I don't want that. You'll have plenty of opportunities to ride when the dudes arrive. Those rides are slower an' a lot safer. I'd feel better if you didn't go."

Sally conceded, although she wasn't happy about it. Pat, Dwight, Scott, and I gathered the broodmares. Scott and I led them in and Dwight and Pat followed. I noticed that Pat had replaced his lariat rope with his bull whip. I also noticed that Dwight was riding his filly.

"Do you think that horse is fast enough to keep up?"

"Why sure," said Dwight.

"Is she fast enough to pass all the others if necessary?" I saw Pat smile when Dwight made the last comment.

"This horse is probably the fastest horse on the place. She's a mustang, remember?"

Pat and I just grinned at Dwight's comment. "Let's hope so," I said.

We brought the broodmare bunch in without incident, although the stud did take after Dwight and his filly and managed to bite the filly. He just nipped the filly; he didn't even break the skin. Pat managed to run him off with the bull whip, after making some buttonholes in his rump. The stud had received this lesson before and it didn't take much for him to remember the lesson.

Sally and Bud were at the corrals when we got there. Sally had built the branding fire and the irons were hot. She'd also brought the camera. We set about branding the colts. Scott and I roped the colts and Pat and Dwight did the ground work.

Before we started branding, Pat roped the stud, took him out of the corral, haltered him and tied him to the fence. The stud had been handled before and even shown in some horse shows. Pat got some salve and doctored the buttonholes he'd put in the horse's rump.

Scott was a little rough on the colts and Bud hollered at him, "Take it easy on them! They're valuable and they're just babies. Don't let them hit the end of the rope so hard!"

Scott was a hand and he immediately became gentler with the colts. I think he really liked to see how high in the air he could "bust" the colts. But he eased off the rough treatment.

We got the colts branded, got all the pictures taken and were ready to take the mares back to their range. Pat turned the stud loose and we headed out. The stud didn't try to take anybody and Pat was careful to warn Dwight not to push them too close.

On the ride back, Dwight said, "You know, that stud nearly got us! I'm glad this horse is as fast as she is; we could have had some real problems."

Pat and I just smiled at Dwight's comment. He hadn't noticed that Pat ran the stud off before he could do much damage. Dwight was real proud of the work he had done with the filly and she was coming along good.

"Do you think Bud will sell this horse to me?" It was clear that Dwight was fond of the horse.

Pat asked, "Which one?"

"This one, of course," said Dwight. "What do you mean which one?"

"If you remember, that filly was runnin' with this stud bunch when we got her. There's a good chance she's pregnant. Everythin' else around this place is," Pat added, looking at me, smiling.

"Yep," I said. "This place is a real baby factory!" I was kinda used to the idea of a soon to be father and kinda proud of it!

Pat and I laughed and Dwight pondered the idea that his filly could be pregnant. Dwight finally said, "I could go for a two for one deal!"

"She's probably pregnant. That 'ol stud is pretty sneaky. That's how we come to have Einstein."

"Who's Einstein?"

"Einstein's that spotted hinny that's followin' the donkey around," said Pat.

"What's a hinny?"

I thought Dwight had more experience and savvy than what he was showing.

Pat explained what a hinny was and how they came about. He finished by saying, "You remember that. The dudes will ask a lot of questions about Einstein this summer. You'll get tired of answerin' the questions."

Bombarded by Dudes

May arrived and the days got warmer. Sally and I picked up the blackboard chart during a trip to town for one of her checkups. As soon as we got back to the ranch and I hung it up on the wall, she started filling in the squares with the names of our guests. When she got done, there wasn't much room. We were booked pretty solid.

Our first guests were due to arrive about the middle of May. We'd already run our saddle horses in and had started riding them. We didn't want any surprises when we put the dudes on them. I was careful not to let Dwight get on anything that might buck. We had a horseshoer come out and shoe the horses. We made arrangements for him to come out about every six weeks to reset the shoes. If a horse threw a shoe, Pat or I could reset it.

My feelings about Dwight were mixed. On some days he was a good hand; on others he seemed pretty green. I made it a point to question him about this later, in private.

Scott was a good hand and he seemed to encourage the horses when they wanted to buck. On the one hand, it might be good to get it out of them as quick as possible; on the other hand, the horse might take to bucking and decide he liked it and keep it up. I decided I'd let things take their course.

Around the first of May, Jim showed up. I don't know why he

kept coming back, apparently he liked the job. I thought he was majoring in resort management or something like that at college.

Sally came to me around the first week in May. "We've got some guests coming in two days," she said.

"Two days! It ain't even the middle of May yet! That's when our first dudes are supposed to be here. What's goin' on?"

"These are extra," said Sally. "They'll only be here a couple of days, but are willing to pay the full rate, so we're going to take them. Its extra money and it'll show up at the end of the year."

"But, Darlin', we ain't runnin' a motel."

"That's what Daddy said. But I've already committed. Missus Abercrombie and I can handle the maid chores, Jim's here, the cook has assured me he's ready and can handle it. You and the boys should have enough horses ready. I think we're set. I'm ready to start making money!"

"I had no idea you were such a money grubbin', money lovin' little wife. I'll tell you what, you make the money an' I'll spend it! How's that sound?"

Sally was excited and ready to get the season started. "You're silly," she said.

"Tell me about the people," I said.

"They're older folks, retired. They told me that they wanted to take their vacation before the roads got crowded. They seem real nice."

"We'll take a look at 'em then see what horses we can put 'em on," I said. "We'll be ready for 'em. Also, it'll give us a chance to show Scott an' Dwight the trails we use before we get busy."

"See! I told you it would be all right," said Sally. She left and she felt good that she could expect a little extra income. She always had the best interest of the ranch, the dudes, and the hired help in mind.

Two days later our first guests, the Caldwell's, showed up. An older couple, they didn't have much interest in riding horses.

However, Mister Caldwell did have an interest in fishing. This presented me with a problem. I didn't fish and knew nothing about it. We hadn't had many requests to go fishing.

I told Bud about the situation. "What kind of fishing does he want? We can take him to some streams on the forest; we'd need to go in the four-wheeler if he doesn't want to go horseback. Or we could take him to the lake. It's about twenty miles away and we could go in the company car. I'll ask him at supper. Let me handle it. I might need to borrow Dwight, depending on where we go."

"Are you a fisherman?"

"I haven't had time to fish for years, but I used to enjoy it. I'll see if I can find some of my old fishing gear. This might be kinda fun. I wonder if I can fish from the four-wheeler?"

"I'll bet you can," I said.

At supper, Mister Caldwell indicated that he'd like to try some stream fishing.

Bud said, "Fine. I know where we can go and we should have some luck. Honey, I'll need to borrow Dwight tomorrow. We're going fishing! Do you want to go fishing, Missus Caldwell? We've got room."

"Gracious no! I'll be very content to relax in this beautiful lodge and read a book."

"If you're goin' fishin'," said Pat, "you've got to catch enough to feed everybody! I think I could probably eat two big ones. How many can you eat Honey?"

"I'd probably settle for two," I said.

Everyone put in their order for how many fish they could eat. The cook also put in his order. "If you're wanting me to cook fish tomorrow, you better bring 'em in cleaned! I ain't cleaning fish."

"That's what we're taking Dwight along for," said Bud. "You ever cleaned a fish, Dwight?"

"Yes sir. I've cleaned plenty."

"Then we're set. We'll leave around six in the morning," said

Bud. "Cookie, if you'll be kind enough to fix us something for dinner tomorrow, I'd appreciate it."

"We'll be home before dinner won't we?" Mister Caldwell had become a little concerned.

"You're thinking supper. Out here the noon meal is dinner and the evening meal is supper. Don't worry, we'll be back in time for supper."

The next morning, Bud, Dwight, and Mister Caldwell left to go fishing while Sally, Pat, Scott, and I gathered the saddle horses. With Missus Caldwell not wanting to go riding, we didn't have much to do other than ride the dude horses.

"Where do you want to ride, Darlin'? We've got our cattle all cared for and in separate pastures, we've been ridin' fence while we been ridin' these dude horses, there ain't much to do other than ride these horses."

"Let's see if we can find Daddy," said Sally. "I have a general idea where he went. It might make for a good ride."

"Whatever you say, Darlin'. Where do you want to ride Pat?"

"I'm thinkin' Scott an I should ride out toward the broodmares."

I gave Pat a look. "You think somethin's goin' on out there?" I immediately had thoughts of the horse thief we'd caught out there last summer.

Pat noticed my concern. "There's nothin' goin on. I just thought it might be nice to ride that direction."

"All right," I said. "Make sure you take a radio, just in case."

Sally saddled her grulla and I saddled one of the dude horses. Pat and Scott saddled their horses and went in the direction of the broodmare band's range. I didn't know where Sally was headed, but apparently she knew where she was going.

It was a pleasant ride and Sally and I visited along the way. She was still excited about her pregnancy and most of our talk concerned the baby.

She asked, "Have you come up with any names?"

"Not really," I answered. "Is it a girl or boy?"

"I don't know," replied Sally. "What do you want?"

"How 'bout just a healthy kid? I'd settle for that," I said.

"We just might have to settle for what we get," said Sally. "Missus Abercrombie has already made some plans. Next time we go to town we need to start picking up some things so we'll be ready."

"What things?"

"We could get a crib, a bassinette, diapers, things like that."

"Don't we need to know what the kid is so we get the right color?"

"Not with those things, Silly."

"You make a list an' we'll go shoppin' when we go to town."

After a few hours we found the fishermen. Mister Caldwell was up stream, in the middle of the stream. He had a look on his face like he was in heaven and appeared to be thoroughly enjoying himself. Dwight was downstream, also in the middle of the stream. Bud was in the four-wheeler, with the front end of the four-wheeler in the stream. It looked like he was stuck. He was so engrossed in his fishing, he didn't notice Sally and I when we rode up.

I hollered, "Havin' any luck?"

Bud was startled. He turned in the four-wheeler and saw us. "Quiet! They'll hear you. Hold on, I think I've got a bite!"

Bud did have a bite and he reeled in what I thought was a large fish for that little stream.

"I didn't know fish had ears," I said. "Looks like you've got a whale there."

"The fishing has been good," said Bud. "This little spot hasn't been fished for some time. I'm glad we haven't over-fished it. We've almost got enough to feed everybody tonight. We only need a few more. Clarence has done the best."

"Clarence?"

"That's Mister Caldwell," said Bud. "He's really a fisherman!"

"Are you stuck, Daddy?" Sally was concerned.

"Just a little bit," said Bud. "We couldn't get it out and decided to fish and then worry about getting unstuck. We were going to call you if we couldn't get free; I've got the two-way radio."

"I think we ought to pull you out while we're here." I took my rope down and called Dwight over. He was so busy fishing, he hadn't noticed us either.

"You've got your hip boots on," I said handing him my rope. "I don't want to get wet. Put this on the frame, then take Sally's rope and tie it to the frame. We'll pull you out right now. Start the motor Bud, you can help."

Dwight put the ropes on the four-wheeler, Bud started it and we pulled it out to dry ground. "Don't get so close to the edge of the stream," I said. "You'll get stuck again. You'll just have to throw your line out there a little farther."

Sally and I decided to leave.

"We'll catch enough fish to feed everyone, then head home," said Bud. "If you make it back before us, alert the cook that we'll be having a fish fry tonight."

The ride back to the ranch was uneventful.

"It's a good thing you wanted to look for them," I said. "They could have been there a while."

"Sometimes I think Daddy is just like a little kid, needing supervision all the time."

"I think he just got a little over excited about fishin'," I said. "He told me he hadn't been fishin' for some time."

"That's what I mean," said Sally. "We might have to hire a person just to go with him and keep an eye on him."

I was surprised at the comment. *A babysitter for Bud!* I knew he wouldn't like that idea, but he really was confined to a wheelchair or the four-wheeler.

"You'd best talk to him about that," I said, not wanting to get too deeply involved.

"I'll mention it to him, but you'll have to back me up!"

"Yes, Darlin', I will."

Pat and Scott and the fishermen made it back to the ranch before Sally and I did. The cook really outdid himself with the fish fry that night. Bud was so pleased with the results of his fishing trip that he contemplated becoming a fishing guide for those guests that wanted to fish.

"I could take a couple of people out in the four-wheeler every few days. We could even charge a little extra for that service."

I had mixed feelings about the idea. Sally like the added income that it might generate, but only agreed to it if Bud consented to take someone from the ranch along with him.

"A babysitter," said Bud.

"If that's what you want to call him," said Sally. "You know Honey and I had to rescue you today."

"If that's what you want, Daughter. Dwight, how would you like to go fishing every few days?"

"I could go for that," said Dwight. "I've guided some fishing and hunting trips before."

"Then that's done," said Pat. "We'll start doing it on a slow basis."

"Make sure you don't schedule it when we're goin' to brand or have somethin' else scheduled," I said. "A lot of our dudes don't want to miss the cowboy activities."

"Yes sir," said Bud.

It appeared that Bud was turning over the operation of the ranch to Sally and me, but still keeping an active part in it.

The Caldwell's left and we started making preparations for the summer guests to start arriving. Before the Caldwell's left, Clarence gave Bud a big tip that he promptly split with Dwight, Sally and me.

"You deserve this," he said handing money to Sally and me. "After all, according to Sally, you rescued us that day!"

I gave my share of the money to Sally. "We'll use this when we start buying the baby things."

Sally, Jim, and Missus Abercrombie were busy making up rooms and cabins.

The Saturday of the middle of May, the guests started to arrive. All at once, there were about fifteen or sixteen dudes on the ranch. Dwight, Scott, Pat, and I were kept busy most of the day carrying suitcases and luggage to the various rooms and cabins after introductions to everyone.

One young couple had a six- or seven-month old baby with them. When I saw Sally, she was holding the youngster.

"You're a little early, aren't you? I didn't think you were due until November," I said. I was trying a little humor.

"Don't be silly, Silly. He's theirs. Isn't he cute?"

"How do you know it's a he?"

"You can tell by the color. Blue is for boys, pink is for girls. Isn't he darling?"

"I guess he's darlin', Darlin'," I said. I got the impression Sally was going to be a good mother. I wasn't surprised—she excelled at everything she did.

I recognized some of the guests from previous years, but some were strangers. I thought I'd have a problem remembering everyone's name, but I'd had the same problems before. I would struggle through it.

Pat had an easier time of it. He remembered the guests that had been here before, their names, and even the horses they'd rode when they were here. He sized up the new guests and I knew he was figuring out what horses to put them on. I was doing the same thing.

We ran in the saddle horses early the next morning and started saddling. We'd find out what riding experience the guests had, then assign them a horse we thought suitable for them. We'd do a little riding instruction in the corral before we went out for a ride. Pat and I had pretty much the same horses in mind for the dudes and the morning went well.

While we were assigning horses, other guests arrived. I sent Dwight and Scott up to help carry luggage in. I told them to tell the new arrivals to get settled and we'd get them horseback after the noon meal if they wanted to go for a ride.

Satisfied that we had our dudes and horses, we took our dudes out for a ride. Pat, Dwight, Scott, Sally, and I accompanied the ride. Sally was leading and the hired help rode along side the dudes.

"This is just like herdin' cows," I told Scott as we rode along.

"Does that mean we can ride up and slap the stragglers on the rump with our bridle reins?" Scott was grinning as he said that and I thought he already knew the answer.

"Certainly not! We need to keep this as safe as possible," I said. I was wondering if Scott might be too much cowboy for the dude business and if he might cause some problems. After all, the last part of "cowboy" is "boy." I made a mental note to discuss the situation with Pat when we could talk in private.

Our ride went well and we returned in time for everyone to get cleaned up for dinner. We were introduced to the new arrivals and made ready to take those that wanted to for a ride after eating. Many of the riders from the morning opted to spend time around the swimming pool. The pool was a very popular place for first time riders after a ride. And the warm afternoons made it even more inviting.

Our first weekend when the dudes arrived was pretty busy. I wanted to keep the dudes busy, if they wanted to stay busy, so at supper that night I announced, "We're goin' to have a brandin' on Tuesday. We'll need about all you folks that want to, to help gather cattle."

"We'll have the cook come out and have a barbeque for our noon meal," said Bud. "If you want to eat dinner, you'll have to be out there or go without. If some of you don't want to go horseback, I can take you out in the four-wheeler."

The announcement caused some excitement among the guests and just about everyone wanted to ride out and help gather cattle.

Doing the Cowboy Thing

On Tuesday, we gathered cattle. We only had about fifty head or so to do this time, so we took our time. When we had the cows and calves corralled, we tied the dude's horses outside the corral and started branding. Sally and I started roping and Sally was just as good as she had been in the past. Pat, Scott, and Dwight made up the ground crew with Pat doing the castrating and ear-marking, Scott doing the branding and vaccinating, and Dwight holding the calves head's down.

Bud had shown up with a few guests in the four-wheeler. Bud stayed out of the corral, his wheelchair making it difficult for him to get around. But he watched what was happening very intently. The cook had shown up and started fixing the barbeque dinner. "This won't take long," said the cook. "When it's ready, just come an' get it."

When we had fifteen or twenty calves branded, I said to Pat, "Here, you rope a few an' I'll do your job. After a while Scott can rope a few, then Dwight. Sally, when you get tired, or hungry, Scott can spell you," I said. Turning to the guests that had been watching, I said, "If any of you folks want to try an' rope somethin', tell me. We'll give you an opportunity. When you get hungry, just go get something to eat. We'll keep brandin' an' we can eat in shifts."

Most of the guests declined the roping, preferring to eat

instead. A few of the younger kids wanted to rope, but I suggested they try back at the ranch where we had some roping dummies set up. That way, if they did catch something, they wouldn't have to worry about dallying up. And I wouldn't have to worry about them getting a finger or a hand caught in the dallies.

One guest wanted to try to rope and Sally promptly rode her horse out of the corral and returned with the guest's horse. As she brought the horse to the guest, I was explaining how to dally, emphasizing the fact that, "You make sure you take your dallies with your thumb up!"

The guest got on his horse and went to rope some calves. He didn't have any success but he did provide a lot of laughs for the other guests. He was somewhat discouraged and willingly gave up his turn at roping.

"That's tiring," he said.

"Yes," I said. "But remember, when you catch one, you get a chance to rest while it's gettin' branded."

The guest laughed. "I'll just rest now. I might never catch one!"

Pat came over after catching a few and volunteered to let Dwight rope a few. "There ain't many left," he said.

Dwight got his horse and entered the corral. He was riding the filly.

"Let's not have a repeat of earlier this year," said Pat. He started to laugh. It was still humorous to him.

"I've been working with her," said Dwight. "She's been getting a lot better. I don't expect any problems."

Dwight and Scott roped the rest of the calves. They came back to the fire.

"I think that's all of them," said Dwight.

"Okay, I'll take a little ride through them just to make sure," I said.

I rode through the small herd and made sure there were no

slicks remaining. Satisfied, I said, "Open the gate Scott, I'll get a count on 'em as they come out."

I counted the cattle as they left the corral and wrote down the number in my tally book. Bud looked satisfied.

"You better eat, Honey. There might be a little left for you."

All the hired help got something to eat and we relaxed a little before heading back to the ranch.

Bud took his riders back in the four-wheeler plus one. A guest thought the ride back might be a little too much for her and managed to squeeze on the four-wheeler. I led her horse back to the ranch.

On the way, Pat dropped back and rode with me.

I asked him, "What do you think of Scott?"

"Oh, he's a good enough hand all right. But we might be losin' him soon. He kinda told me in a roundabout way that he wanted to rodeo some, an' this might be a little tame for him. He told me he'd talk to you when he made up his mind."

"Just to be on the safe side, I better start lookin' through some of our old applications. If we don't get someone, we'll be short-handed. I think Bud is figurin' on takin' Dwight with him on his fishin' excursions. Sally was thinkin' we ought to get someone to go with him every time he left in the four-wheeler anyway. That's goin' to leave only you an' me essentially. I don't want Sally to do much ridin' bein' pregnant. I suppose I should hire an extra man even if Scott does stay around."

"That might be prudent," said Pat.

"Prudent? What do you mean?"

"Well," said Pat, "at least I didn't say pregnant!"

We both laughed and continued to ride to the ranch.

That night I started to look at the applications from the people we didn't hire.

Sally noticed and asked, "What are you doing?"

I told Sally what Pat and I had discussed that afternoon.

"I think it's still early enough that we might still be able to get some good help. I'll have to give it a try or we'll be short-handed. You better look at these with me an' help me make up my mind."

We went over the applications together and I made a few calls to individuals we thought might be suitable and still available. Sally remembered a lot of the applicants from the interviews at the college and indicated which ones I should and shouldn't call.

I spent the next few evenings on the phone trying to hire some help. Most of the people I called had already accepted positions elsewhere. I was becoming a little discouraged.

Bud had been informed of our possible dilemma, and he told me, "You need to go to Scott and find out what his plans are! He can't hold this over our heads like this. We need a commitment from him."

"We'll just let it play out," I said.

"I swear," said Bud, "you're easier going than I am!"

"That's why you've been so hard to live with over the years," said Sally, giving her dad a hug.

Bud just laughed. "We can cut out the fishing if we have to. But I was really looking forward to it."

"We won't cut out anythin'," I said. "What's the 'ol cowboy sayin'? 'When the goin' gets tough, the tough get goin'.' We'll work through this one way or another. You go fishin' an' get enough so you can feed everybody."

I finally found someone that hadn't got a job yet. His name was Chuck Hill. I told him, "You show up here in a couple of days. We'll hire you on a trial basis for a week; provide you with room an' board an' a wage. After a week, if you work out, we'll hire you for the summer. If you don't work out, we'll let you go, no hard feelings. Is that fair?"

"That's more than fair," he said. "I'll be there tomorrow, before dark, barring any car problems."

"Bring everything you need, a saddle, bedding an' extra clothes, an' anythin' else you might need."

"Yes sir."

I told the cook that they would be an extra mouth to feed tomorrow. "You know we always have plenty," he said, "but I appreciate you telling me."

I also told Sally I'd hired another person. "That's good. Daddy wants to go fishing."

"Tell him to wait one day. Then we can send Dwight with him."

The next day, Chuck Hill showed up. It was about supper time. He was about like I'd expected, around eighteen, but with some pretty fair experience behind him. I met him at the lodge and made introductions all around.

"We'll eat, then I'll show you where to put your stuff."

The next day we had Chuck ride one of the dude horses that didn't get used much. His saddle was old as was his bridle, but they were both serviceable. His saddle pads and blankets were about worn out. He knew how to ride.

I gave him a saddle blanket and pad. "Use these," I said. "Your's are about worn out."

He thanked me, then got on his horse, cheeking him. Not many people knew what cheeking was and few could do it and get on as gracefully as he did. *We might have a hand here,* I thought.

I noticed Pat's silent approval as he watched Chuck.

"You don't have to cheek these horses," I told him. "They've all been rode this year an' they're all fairly gentle."

"Yes sir," he said.

An' you don't have to keep callin' me sir," I said. "Although it's about time I got the respect I truly deserve. I answer to Honey."

I saw Pat smile at my last comment, but he didn't say anything.

Chuck gave me a funny look and said, "Yes sir … ah, that is Honey. Honey?" He questioned the nickname.

I noticed his look and said, "Ask my wife."

We took the dudes that wanted to ride out to move cows around in preparation for our next branding. It was part of our regular pasture rotation program. I watched Chuck most of the morning and he appeared to know what he was doing. He was also very courteous to the guests, whereas Scott was a little sullen and abrupt with the guests. I made up my mind that we'd keep him, but didn't tell him.

I also thought that I should confront Scott and find out what his plans were now that we had all our bases covered. I checked with Pat to make sure that it was all right with him that I confront Scott. I didn't want Scott thinking that Pat had ratted on him.

Pat assured me it was all right. "We have to do what's best for the ranch," he said.

That night while we were unsaddling at the barn, I asked Scott, "What are your plans? I understand you might think this is a little tame for you."

"I have been thinking about leaving and doing some rodeoing. And this is fairly slow. I'd like a little more action."

"You can do what you want," I said. "But you need to let me know what your plans are so we can adjust. That's only fair."

When pressed a little, Scott became a little nervous. "I guess I'll move on," he said.

"When?"

"What's best for you?"

I thought it would be best if he left right away, but didn't say anything. I didn't want it to look like we were running him off; he was the son of a friend of Bud's.

I asked him, "Why don't you help out until Sunday night. You can leave after supper. I'll have Sally make out your check an' have it ready then."

"That'll work," he said. He looked somewhat relieved.

After supper, Sally, Bud, Pat, and I were visiting in the kitchen.

I told Sally and Bud about the discussion I'd had with Scott.

Pat asked, "How come you're havin' him stay so long? He's ready to leave now."

"That was an inspiration," I said, feeling kinda proud of myself. "We have a whole lot of guests leaving on Saturday and a whole bunch comin' in on Sunday. I thought it might be a good idea to keep him around to help carry luggage! They'll be plenty!"

"I like your thinking!" said Bud.

"Me too," added Pat.

"Make sure someone's down at the barn when he loads his stuff," said Bud.

"Shades of the 'ol days?" Pat was grinning when he asked the question.

"Yes," said Bud.

I had to ask, "Shades of the 'ol days. What do you mean?"

"We had one feller leave sorta prematurely an' he took five or six of our saddles with him," said Pat. "When Bud noticed they were missin' he stopped him before he got out of the yard by sayin' somethin' about gettin' his bonus check. The feller naturally stopped an' Bud pulled him out of his car. I thought he was goin' to kill him before I could get 'em separated. We opened the trunk an' sure enough, there were our saddles. We'd just bought 'em, they'd only been used part of the summer, some of 'em still squeaked."

I could see Bud was enjoying Pat's telling of the story; he was enjoying a good laugh. "The guy hasn't been back since," said Bud. "Just make sure one of you guys are at the barn when he loads his stuff. You can tell him how much you'll miss him or something."

Apparently Bud didn't have any qualms about me forcing Scott's hand, he didn't say anything.

"I'll make sure you're on a ride or somethin', Pat. Then you won't have to help carry luggage. Scott, Dwight, Chuck, an' I will handle that, an' I'll make sure Scott gets more than his share."

Bud and Pat laughed. "You're starting to think like a foreman," said Bud. "I like that."

"I don't know if I do," said Pat.

We all laughed and considered the matter done. All that remained was to get as much work out of Scott as possible before he left.

Most of the guests were leaving Saturday, but there were a few staying on for the second week. I had Pat take them riding, and explained that the rest of us would have to help carry bags for the departing guests.

Bud came out to tell everyone goodbye and invite them back the following year. As I was going back to the lodge to get some more luggage, Bud called me over.

"I really don't have anything to say, Honey. I thought you might like a break from being a bellboy. We'll act like we're discussing something."

"I like your thinkin'," I said. "You're really teachin' me how to think like management!"

Bud laughed. "We do have to look out after our own. Make sure you invite everybody back! It's how we make a living."

Sally was busy with Missus Abercrombie and Jim cleaning up rooms for the guests that were coming tomorrow, but she did manage to come and tell everyone goodbye. She looked a little tired and I asked her, "Do you need some help? I could come an' give you a hand."

"No," she said, "we're cleaning these rooms. I'm sure if you tried to help, we'd have a bigger mess to clean up than what we started with."

She smiled as she said that and winked at me as she started to leave.

"I do appreciate your consideration though," she said. "The

new maids we hired should start arriving next week. It'll get easier then."

"You know," I said, "as foreman, I'm supposed to keep abreast of everythin'. I'm just doin' my job."

"And a good job you're doing!"

I visited with Bud and watched Scott, Dwight, and Chuck carry luggage to the guests' vehicles. Dwight and Chuck didn't seem to mind, but I could tell Scott was not really happy. I thought his leaving might be for the best.

As I watched the proceedings, my mind wandered back over the wranglers we'd had in the past. We'd really been fortunate; we'd hired some good people. There was Jeff, Dave, and Jim, from three years ago, or was it four? It was hard for me to keep track. There was also Richard and Jason from last year. None of these guys showed any displeasure in assisting the guests as Scott was displaying at this time.

I told Bud, "Since I've been here we've only had one out of eight wranglers not work out good. That's not too bad an average, but it's still too high."

"Honey, you'll find that most of our applicants aren't over qualified. We like to hire the college-aged kids. Even though they don't have the horse experience, they seem to get along with the guests better than the old cowboys, although the older cowboys have more horse experience. Of course, we can teach the younger people what they need to know to get along here, but I keep looking for people like you and Pat. You've both got the necessary horse experience and your personalities are such that you can get along good with the dudes. I'm thinking Dwight might be along the same lines. Maybe Chuck also. It remains to be seen. Scott might have too much ego, like most young cowboys, to be really good at the dude business."

I resolved to exercise more judgment in the future when it came to hiring wranglers.

"The inseminator is coming next week to start breeding the heifers," said Bud. "Where are you going to put him up? I think Sally said all our accommodations are full."

"Sally and I talked about this earlier, he'll have to stay in the bunkhouse, there's plenty of room there. I thought I'd help pull the bullers an' Pat can handle the rides. I was thinkin' Scott might pull the bullers, but he'll be gone."

Scott came up to me after supper and said, "There have been some things come up and I probably ought to leave tonight."

I thought it was strange; he hadn't had a phone call. I thought it was just a ploy to get away early. I knew he didn't like playing a bellboy.

I didn't question him about it. I thought if he wanted to leave, it would be better to let him go now rather than try to get another day's work out of him.

"Okay," I said. "I'll have Pat help you load your stuff while I get your check."

I called Pat over and told him Scott was leaving that night and asked him, "Would you mind givin' him a hand loadin' his stuff?"

Pat gave me a knowing look and said, "Surely." He knew what I had in mind.

Scott got his gear, I gave him his check, and he left.

"That's over," I told Pat.

"Don't fret on it none," he said. "Over the years there's been a lot leave, just like that. One guy was in such a rush to get away, he didn't even pick up his check. Bud had to send it to his last known address an' it was returned. I think Bud still has it up in the office."

"What do you think of the two hands we still have?"

"I think they'll be all right. But it remains to be seen."

The next day, Pat took the morning ride and the new guests started arriving. Dwight, Chuck, and I were busy doing the bellboy chores. Bud called me over again to get acquainted with the arriving guests, and as soon as I met them, I went back to carrying luggage. I did feel a little guilty about not helping today, although I didn't feel guilty yesterday.

We soon had all the guests moved into their quarters and I asked if anyone wanted to go riding. There were a few people that wanted to go and I told them we'd be down at the corrals. They showed up, we assigned horses, adjusted stirrups, gave a little basic riding instruction, and went for a ride. Sally, Dwight, Chuck, and I took the ride. I gave Pat the rest of the day off.

He smiled and went to the bunkhouse and took a nap.

During the day, the girls that Sally and Bud had hired as maids started to show up. I was relieved to see them, it would make Sally's job easier. Jim and Missus Abercrombie could handle most of the training of the new help and Sally could take it a little easier, if I could convince her to.

That evening the inseminator showed up. He was scheduled to stay for forty-five days. I went to the calving pens where we were keeping the yearling replacement heifers and started to look for the bullers.

Later that night, I told Pat that he would have to have Dwight and Chuck help him run in the saddle horses; I'd have to pull the bullers in the morning.

"We can handle that," he said. "What you goin' to have Sally do?"

"You know Sally," I said, "she'll do whatever she wants to. I'd prefer to have her help me. It'll be a little safer for her, maybe easier too!"

Sally did come down and help pull the bullers. We had ten or twelve heifers for the inseminator to breed. We'd do that in the afternoon.

When we returned to the lodge, Dwight was bringing in a solitary horse. The rider was walking about fifty yards behind the horse. I rode up to Dwight. A rider walking back to the ranch usually meant trouble and serious trouble at that.

"What's wrong?"

"This lady is allergic to horses," answered Dwight. "Pat sent me back with her. I think she's all right, as long as she stays away from the horses."

Sally gave me her horse and walked toward the woman. She was careful to stay away from the woman, as Sally had horse all over her. "If you go to your room and take a shower, you should be all right. Put your clothes outside your room. I'll gather them up and wash them."

"That's not necessary," said the woman. "I just forgot to take my allergy medicine. I'll be all right as soon as I get it."

"Are you sure?"

"Yes," said the guest. "This has happened before, I'll be all right."

Sally returned to where Dwight and I were taking care of her horse. "It's okay. She's allergic to horses, and she's dealt with this before. I'll check on her in a little bit."

"I've never heard of someone being allergic to horses," said Dwight.

"Neither have I, but I guess it's possible. There's livin' proof."

"We run into a lot of strange things here, don't we?"

"Yes," I said and was tempted to add, *and the strangest are the people themselves*, but decided to keep quiet. I didn't need to be influencing Dwight in anything but a positive manner and I wasn't sure how positive my comment or thought might be.

When Pat returned, his first question was, "How's the woman? Did they make it back okay? She assured me she had ridden quite a bit in the past an' that she'd just forgot to take her allergy medicine."

"That's what Sally told me after she talked to the woman," I said. "She's at the lodge now washin' her clothes. I think she'll be all right. We might want to check with her each day an' make sure she took her medicine."

"Another chore," said Pat. "You allergic to anythin'?"

"Not that I know of," I said. "How about you?"

"Yeah," said Pat. "I got some allergies, work bein' one of 'em, but I haven't found a medicine to cure that!"

I laughed. "You probably won't."

"But I'll keep lookin' for one!"

We both laughed and went to unsaddling horses.

Breaking the Routine

Sally continued to help me pull the bullers morning and evening. I didn't get a chance to go out with the dudes much because I was looking for bullers and operating the squeeze chute. The replacement heifer program had become almost a full time job.

When we had to do some branding, I'd generally miss the gathering part of the day and show up after the cattle had been corralled. I'd rope a few calves just to have some fun and stay in shape, then leave early to run the squeeze chute for the inseminator. Then I'd ride and look for bullers toward evening.

Pat suggested one day, "Maybe you ought to let one of us take care of the heifers an' you go out with the dudes. They say a change is as good as a vacation."

"I'll have to do somethin', Sally needs to go to the doc's for a checkup an' she wants me to take her. Who do you think would do the best at pullin' bullers, Dwight, Chuck, or yourself?"

"Me? Why include me in that?"

"You said it, 'a change is as good as a vacation.' I'm not so sure either Dwight or Chuck could do as good a job as you would. They've got pretty good at keepin' an eye on the dudes."

"I'll do it if you want," said Pat.

When I had to take Sally to the doctor's, Pat handled the replacement heifer chores. Dwight and Chuck took the dudes out for scenic rides. Bud went down to the barn to watch and offer advice if necessary.

On the way to town, I asked Sally, "When are you goin' to give up ridin'?"

"What?" She sounded surprised.

"Well, Darlin'," I said, thinking I might have opened a can of worms, "I've noticed your pregnancy is really showin' an' it's gettin' difficult for you to get on your horse. I was thinkin' it might be easier on you if you didn't ride until after the baby was born."

"You're right about getting on my horse," she said. "I've been considering using the mounting block. And I am getting big enough; I almost don't fit in the saddle. I might have to stop riding. But how would you handle everything without me helping out?"

Mustering up all the diplomacy I could gather, I said, "It would be a little tough, but we'd do it somehow. We'd have to ask more of Pat, Dwight, and Chuck. Of course, I'd have to do more also. But I'd feel better if you stopped ridin' 'til after the baby's born. You're big enough that you're even havin' difficulty takin' your dallies when you rope calves."

"I noticed that at the last branding," said Sally. "And it is getting a little uncomfortable. Maybe I will stop. Will you ride my horses, just to keep them in shape?"

"I thought you wanted to be the only one to ride the grulla."

"That's right, but they still need to be kept in shape. I'd feel comfortable if I knew you were riding them and not somebody else," she said.

"I'll do it, but only for you an' only if you insist. That's a good idea to stop ridin'," I said. "If you want to join in on some of the activities, you can come out with Bud in the four-wheeler or use the golf cart. It ain't got any use since Bud got the four-wheeler. I'll make sure it's plugged in when we get back. It'll be ready for you in the mornin'."

After the checkup at the doctor's and finding out everything was normal, we did some shopping. Sally picked out a crib, a bassinet, some diapers, and other miscellaneous items like baby powder, she thought she'd need. She really enjoyed shopping for the baby even though she didn't know whether it was a boy or girl.

She'd look at an item, then say, "I'll buy this after I find out if it's a boy." She wanted everything to be perfect.

I looked at the baby powder she'd bought and said, "Better get more of that. You know it's real good for stoppin' the squeakin' in the stirrup leathers on new saddles."

"It's for the baby, Silly! You men are sometimes so disgusting!" But she'd be smiling when she said that.

We got something to eat and started to go back to the ranch. I asked Sally if she wanted to take in a movie, but she declined. We got back to the ranch in time for supper.

I went to the calving sheds to see how the inseminator was doing and met Pat.

"We got nine heifers bred," said Pat, "an' I've got the ear tag numbers on some that will be ready to breed tomorrow. This is really pretty easy duty, there's no questions to answer, there's no requests to sing an' there's no stress worrin' about the dudes fallin' off. You've actually had somewhat of a vacation here, haven't you?"

"Sure," I said. "It's been a real picnic." I took the paper with the numbers on it from Pat.

"I did check on the boys at noon, an' their rides this mornin' an' everythin' went all right. I haven't been back to the barn yet to see how everythin' went this afternoon. They even told me they checked on the woman with allergies an' made sure she'd taken her medicine. She had. The boys do pay attention to detail. Which one are you thinkin' of keepin' through the winter?"

"Actually, I was thinkin' of keepin' both of 'em, if they want to stay. Sally wants to have someone accompany Bud everywhere, his condition ain't gettin' any better an' Dwight might do all right there. Chuck don't seem to mind doin' anythin'. An' an extra hand would make our job a little easier."

"You know, you're really givin' this some thought, aren't you?"

"Just part of the job," I said, "just part of the job. I'll check for bullers in the mornin', unless you've decided you like this so much you want to continue doin' it."

"You can do it. I sorta like ridin' out in the open rather than bein' confined in a feedlot."

"I thought so," I said.

On Saturday, Pat volunteered to help out with the bellboy duties. We drew straws to see if Dwight or Chuck would take out the few riders that were remaining and wanted to ride. Chuck won and I told Dwight he could take out the riders on Sunday. There seemed to be a real sense of fairness and fair play among the wranglers and I really appreciated that.

Sally was able to spend more time with the departing guests. Jim and Missus Abercrombie had done a good job of training the new maids and they were busy cleaning the rooms and cabins in preparation for the guests that would be arriving Sunday.

As I was saying goodbye to some of the guests, Sally came up to me with a triumphant look on her face.

"We made a mistake," she said after the guests had left.

"Oh?" I couldn't understand the look on Sally's face and a mistake at the same time. "What did we do wrong?"

"We didn't do anything wrong, we just didn't do enough."

"With regard to what?" I wasn't following Sally's line of thinking.

"We need another board to put reservations on for next year. I've been inviting the guests back for next year as they've paid their bill and some of them have made reservations and even given me a deposit. We need another board. I wasn't thinking when we made up the first one. If I'd have been thinking, we'd have made up two to start with."

Sally sounded a little disgusted with herself at this apparent oversight.

Bud had overheard the conversation and said, "That's good, Daughter. Get one next time you go to town! We must be doing something right!"

Sally was pleased. She also asked, "How long do you want to operate the dude deal into September? I've had some requests for lodging and such into September. I haven't firmed up on anything yet; I wanted to check with you before I did anything."

"What's our hired help situation in September? You know, we can't cut ourselves short and still provide the service that I want," said Bud. "We have a good reputation and I want to maintain it. That's why we have such a high return rate."

"We'll have Pat," I said. "An' I've been thinkin' of keepin' Dwight an' Chuck through the winter, but haven't discussed it with them. Right now, I don't know what their plans are. What is our maid situation?"

"Jim has graduated from college," said Sally. "He's applied at some ski areas for work, but hasn't heard anything yet. If he gets hired at one of them, he won't start until November. I've talked to him and he's indicated to me that he's available into October. We'll be losing our maids when school starts. We won't have that many guests and he's assured me that he can handle everything. I can help him of course. I think we should extend our season into the end of September or the first of October. What do you think?"

Bud said, "Do you think we can handle it?" His question was directed at both Sally and me.

"I know we can," said Sally. "That's why I'm bringing it up."

"I think we can," I said. "Maybe we can hire a woman from town to help with the maid chores in September. I'll also have to talk to Dwight an' Chuck an' see what they've got planned. We can probably do it."

"Just look at the extra income it will generate," said Sally.

"If you're sure you can do it," said Bud, "go ahead. You know I won't be of any help. You'll be on your own."

"We can do it!" Sally was positive.

In order to stay on top of things, I talked to Dwight and Chuck that night in the bunkhouse. I noticed that Dwight had thrown his hat on the bed and his spurs were on the floor.

"Don't you know that it's bad luck to put your hat on the bed?"

"Oh really," said Dwight, putting his hat on his head. "I didn't know that."

"Yeah," I said. "It would be better to put your hat on the floor an' your spurs on the bed. It would sure make gettin' out of bed in the mornin' easier an' a lot less painful."

I was teasing Dwight a little and having some fun. We visited for a short while before I got down to the main purpose for my visit.

"Both of you guys have been doin' a real good job here," I said. "I'd be interested in knowin' what your plans are for the winter. We have some plans on extending our business but before we proceed, I'd like to know what your plans are."

Neither one of the boys said anything and I became concerned that my plans might become interrupted. But, each one of the boys was waiting for the other one to speak first.

Finally, I said, "Dwight, what are your plans?"

Prompted, Dwight replied, "I really don't have any. I was sorta hoping I could stay on here, if you've got work during the winter. I'm open."

"Chuck?"

"I kinda feel like Dwight. I haven't got anything planned."

"Well, boys, I'd like to keep you both on during the winter.

Dwight, I thought you could give Bud a hand when he needed it, along with helpin' with the regular ranch chores."

Dwight asked, "What will our ranch chores be during the winter?"

"We'll have to feed the cows, of course. An' we'll have the replacement heifers to take care of in the feedlot. We'll have colts to halter break an' we'll start breakin' the comin' two-year-olds. We can stay pretty busy. But it will have to be done every day, regardless of the weather or how cold it gets. If you want to stay on for the winter, I'd like to know now an' I'll expect a commitment. I don't want to count on somebody then have 'em quit like Scott did. You can take a couple of days an' think it over then let me know."

"I can tell you right now," said Dwight. "I'm good for the winter and at this point, next summer too!"

"Me too," said Chuck.

In an effort to impress upon them just how important this was, I shook hands with both of them. "We'll count on it," I said.

I told Sally that both Dwight and Chuck had consented to stay on through the winter and the following summer. I was quite pleased with myself. We wouldn't have to worry about hiring and training any new wranglers in the spring.

"But, I would like to hire a woman from town for September," I said, "just to help you out. I'm afraid you're wearin' yourself pretty thin."

"Thin? Haven't you noticed Honey? I'm gaining weight!" I knew she was teasing me at her own expense.

"Ah … well … you see … that's ah … well, that's sorta expected during pregnancy, ain't it?" Sally could still get me stammering and stuttering.

She laughed. "Yes it is," she said. "But I know what you mean. We'll see what we can do in September."

I resolved to call the employment office in August.

The summer was slowly passing. Each week we had guests leaving on Saturday and guests arriving on Sunday. We had completed the artificial breeding program and turned the Angus bull in with the heifers.

"He might not have a lot of work to do," I told Pat. "I hope he can cover those heifers that didn't cycle or didn't catch. I'll check with Bud an' see what he wants to do with him in thirty days. If he keeps him, we might have some black bally calves on the ground next spring."

With our breeding program done for the year, I had more time to spend with the dudes. Pat, Dwight, and Chuck had done well while I was occupied with the heifers and I had forgotten how stressful handling the dudes actually was. I was a little relieved when I had to take Sally in for her next checkup.

I brought the company car around to take Sally to town.

"That won't do," she said.

"What?"

"We'll need your truck. We've got to pick up our new reservation board on the way back. It won't fit in the car."

"Oh," I said. "You didn't tell me."

"But I planned it all out. I called yesterday, it's ready." I was sometimes amazed at Sally's efficiency. Rarely was there a wasted motion or thought.

On our way to town, Sally and I were talking. "You've spent a lot more time with the smaller kids this year than last," she said.

I had spent a lot of my free time while we were breeding heifers with the younger kids and Matilda. The kids really enjoyed Matilda, and Einstein was making a big hit with them.

"Yes, I've had more free time since hirin' Chuck. I generally get done with the heifers too late to be of any help with the dudes an' have to start too early in the afternoon. It's about the only place I can be an' still feel like I'm doin' somethin' worthwhile."

"Daddy noticed that and told me you were having a good time with the kids."

"Yes, I have been having a good time with them. I've actually been usin' the kids for practice."

"For practice? What do you mean?"

"It should be obvious, especially to you. You're pregnant; I'm goin' to be a father. I ain't never been a father before an' don't know how to act. I thought I'd practice on other people's kids before I had to practice on my own. That makes sense, doesn't it? Makes sense to me."

Sally was laughing. "If you say so! Get it right on other people's kids so you'll know what to do with yours. That's pretty sneaky."

"I just think it's smart," I said.

When we returned to the ranch, with the new reservation board, Chuck helped me carry it in and hang it. When it was hung on the wall, Sally went right to work entering the reservations she'd made for the following year. She'd had her reservations made on pieces of paper and she was clearly relieved when they were all posted on the board.

It was time to do another branding. We'd done some while I was busy with the heifers, but it was time to do another one. I announced it one night at supper and the next day. "We'll have a barbeque out there for dinner. Those of you that don't want to help gather cattle can ride out with either Bud or Sally. They'll be takin' the four-wheeler an' golf cart."

I was becoming used to the routine and assuming more responsibility with regards to the operation of the ranch and also the dude aspect.

The next day we gathered cattle and branded without incident. I counted cows out of the corral.

"According to my count, we're about half done brandin'," I said to Bud. "Does that figure with your ideas?"

"I think we're right on schedule," he said. "This has worked out fine so far, I can't find anything wrong."

"Well, we'll just keep doin' what we've been doin'. We do need to start plannin' for our horse sale."

As we talked, we ate the barbeque.

"I think we'll put off our horse sale another year. We had some good success with the last one, but the weaners didn't bring as much as I would have liked. If we put the sale off a year, we can sell coming two- and three-year-olds as started ranch colts, and sell a few of the yearlings, particularly the fillies. We'll keep the weaners until they're started as two-year-olds; they will bring a better price. Remind me to tell Sally that our next sale will be a year from now. She can put it in her newsletter," Bud said.

"I heard that," said Sally. "We'll get a calendar and figure out when to hold the sale when we get back to the ranch."

"While we're talkin," I said, "what do you want to do with the Angus bull, keep him or take him to the sale?"

"Let's keep him. We'll figure out what to do with him this fall. He may have found a home here for a while," Bud replied.

The following few days were spent moving cattle around in our pasture rotation program. We did a good job of keeping those dudes busy that wanted to stay busy.

I got to looking at the overall operation of the ranch and trying to figure out where we could improve. I did have an idea and presented it to Bud one night after supper.

"I think we ought to invest in a small front end loader an' a truck with a manure spreader on the back. The people we hired last year charged us too much to clean our corrals an' they hauled the manure to their own hay fields. We could clean our own corrals an' spread the manure on our own meadows an' grassland. We'd save money in the long run an' improve our grass production. What do you think?"

Bud pondered the question for a while. "I'm glad you're

talking to me about manure spreading after supper rather than during supper. What do you figure it would cost us to get the equipment?"

"I haven't priced the stuff," I said. "I have no idea."

"How small a front end loader?"

"I think they call 'em Bobcats or Skidsters or something like that. I don't know what they cost; I've seen 'em at the machinery company. I've also seen 'em at the lumberyard."

"Do you stay up nights thinking of these things?"

"Not really," I said. "But, I'm always kinda thinkin' on how we can improve things. Sally ain't the only one that thinks around here. I just don't come up with as many good ideas as she does."

Bud laughed. "When you take her to town, take some time and check out the prices. When we have more information, we can make an informed, intelligent decision. You might be on to something here."

During the next trip to town, after Sally's checkup we went to the machinery company to check out prices. These pieces of equipment were more expensive than I thought. I also checked on how much it would cost to equip a truck with a bed fitted as a manure spreader. The idea wasn't new to the machinery people. They had brochures showing just what I wanted. The only problem was that they were all mounted on new trucks. I knew the cost would be prohibitive.

I told the salesperson that I already had a truck; I just wanted the box with the manure spreader fittings. The salesperson left and returned shortly with some figures.

"If you already have the truck, we can fit the box to it."

I thanked the salesman and we left with all the printed information we could get.

I told Sally of my ideas on the way home. "Do you think Bud will go for it?" I asked.

"I don't know. He's pretty much turned over the operation of the ranch to us. If we press him, he'll go for it. Let me see those figures," she said.

Sally looked over the figures on the way home. "This stuff does cost a pretty penny. No wonder those people charged us so much to clean corrals. I know what they charged, I wrote out the check!"

"The only benefit we'll get from it this year will be increased grass production next year. I suppose that's not a benefit this year. I guess the only way we can measure that is by comparing the weaning weights each year. I think it will pay in the long run. An' of course we'll be able to use it year after year. I think it's a good idea."

"We'll see what Daddy says. I think you're right!"

"I have duly noted that you have agreed with me!"

We both laughed and drove to the ranch.

Sally and I presented the costs to Bud the next day. He appeared interested, but didn't commit. "Next time you go to town, I'll go with you and look over this equipment."

We continued our dude activities. Dwight and Chuck did well with the guests, answering the same questions from different individuals each day. I was able to spend more time riding with the tourists and figuring out activities to keep them busy. As we rode, I noted the grasslands and meadows where I thought the manure would do the most good.

I discussed my idea with Pat and he seemed in favor of it.

"Will we have to harrow that freshly spread manure?"

"I don't know. We'll have to see how good the spreader works. If the manure comes out in big chunks, yes. If it comes out finer, probably not."

Towards the end of July, I had to take Sally to town for another checkup. Bud came with us and after Sally's visit to the doc, we went to the machinery company.

As I unloaded Bud's motorized wheelchair, I noticed the

salesman watching us. I wondered what he was thinking as he watched. We went inside and the salesman greeted us. Bud said, "What can you tell me about these Bobcats or Skidsters?"

The salesman told Bud pretty much the same thing he'd told me and Sally earlier. Then he volunteered, "Would you like to drive one?"

"How can I drive one? I'm sorta confined to this wheelchair."

"That's the beauty of these. You handle them with your hands. I'll bring out a demo and let you operate it. I think you'll like it."

He left and returned shortly driving a Skidster. He gave a little demonstration on how it worked, then got out and invited Bud to operate it.

Bud was a little reluctant, but eventually got in. The salesman explained the starting, stopping, and turning of the unit.

Tentatively, Bud started the unit. It was fairly simple. Hand controls started it, turned it, and even backed it up. Hand controls also managed the bucket. After Bud became a little comfortable, he relaxed and gave the unit a good test drive. When he was satisfied, he said, "Honey, you give this a whirl. It's actually a little fun."

I climbed in, the salesman gave me instructions, and I started out tentatively, like Bud, but I soon became comfortable.

Bud told the salesman, "We need to talk this over some."

The salesman left and I asked Bud, "What do you think?"

"That's really some machine! It might work pretty good for cleaning our corrals. We might also use it for some snow removal during the winter. I'll go talk to them. Give me that information you brought."

I gave Bud all the printed information I had on the Skidster and manure trucks and he went into the salesman's office. Sally and I visited outside.

"He looked like he was havin' fun, didn't he?"

"Yes," answered Sally. "Just like a kid in a toy store."

Presently, Bud called us in. "I think we've bought a Skidster," he said. "Now, what did you have in mind for a truck to haul manure?"

"I thought we could change the bed on the two-ton an' make it into a manure hauler," I said.

"That truck's too good to convert it now. Let's go see what kind of used outfits we can find to do this."

The salesman said, "We have an older two-ton truck that we could convert."

"Let's take a look at it." Apparently, Bud liked my idea and was serious about it.

We looked at the truck. "It'll do for a manure spreader," said Bud. "How's it run."

"Take her for a spin," said the salesman.

"Honey, that'll be your job."

I took the truck out. It seemed to run all right. The whole experience reminded me of when my dad bought me my truck as an early Christmas present.

I reported to Bud that the truck seemed to be all right.

"If we can reach a price, we'll get it," said Bud. "Get my checkbook. You kids come in here. We might get this done today."

Bud ended up buying the truck and having the manure spreading box installed. He was assured it would be ready in a few days. Part of the deal included having the Skidster and truck delivered to the ranch.

Four days later, the Skidster and manure spreader arrived. Bud was quite pleased. Pat looked at the Skidster with skepticism.

"Who's goin' to run that?"

"I know how to run that," said Dwight. "I've run one before."

"Good," said Bud. "Can you run that truck?"

"Yes," said Dwight.

"Honey, you've got your corral cleaning and manure hauling

crew. I'll run the Skidster and Dwight can run the truck. You tell him where you want the manure spread and how to get there. We'll handle the rest. We'll get started tomorrow, first thing."

The next day, the corral cleaning crew got started. On our first ride of the morning, we went out by way of the feedlot. Bud was busy scraping the corrals and didn't notice us as we rode by, at a distance.

"It looks like Bud is really goin' after that," said Pat.

"Yep. He may secretly be a frustrated heavy equipment operator," I said.

At the noon meal, Bud came in elated. "We've almost got the feedlot pens cleaned. We're doing this faster than the people we hired to do it last year. We'll be done with it tomorrow. This might be the best idea we've had yet!"

"Are you having fun, Daddy?"

"Yes Daughter, yes!" It was plain that Bud was excited about this project.

After dinner, Sally said, "That was a real good idea, having Daddy clean the corrals. That has given him some purpose and improved his outlook considerably. I think he was beginning to feel useless here."

"That wasn't my idea," I said. "Your father kinda took it on himself. It does look like he's havin' fun though."

Bud and Dwight finished cleaning the feedlot the next day.

At supper, I asked, "Did you get the alleyways?" I was half way teasing, but Bud took me serious.

"Most assuredly! It's cleaner now than when we had it built. Tomorrow we'll start on the horse corrals. We might even go out and clean the branding corrals. I might even take it and smooth out the four-wheeler path to the branding corrals. I've got a lot of projects in mind for that little piece of equipment."

I said, "I take it you're satisfied with this idea?"

"Satisfied? I'm elated. We should have done this a long time ago!"

"Yes," said Sally, "just look at all the fun you've been missing out on all this time." Sally was having fun with her father.

"Fun? Daughter, this is work! And Dwight and I are making progress on it."

"Dwight," I asked, "how are you holding up under this flurry of excitement?"

"I'm doing okay. Only Bud tends to wake me up when he bumps the truck with the Skidster! It's really difficult to get my proper rest!"

We all laughed. I could see that Dwight was fitting in well with Bud. It took some familiarity to joke with the owner of the ranch as Dwight did.

"Dwight," said Bud, "I'm only bumping the truck to keep you awake! You can't be sleeping while I'm working like the dickens!"

We all laughed again.

"Bud," I said, "if you're bumpin' that new Skidster into that new manure spreader, I might have to come out there an' supervise that operation! Just because that's a manure spreader doesn't mean it has to look like one in the first week we have it. You might have to be a little more careful!"

"Yes sir," said Bud. "I'll certainly be more careful in the future!"

Once again we laughed and soon retired for the evening.

Before going to bed, Sally told me, "I'm really happy to see how Daddy has taken to this new project. He's actually enjoying it and I haven't seen him laugh so much in a long time. And just think, it's the dirtiest job on the place. "

"It's given him something to do. He feels like he's got a purpose now. Tomorrow, when he's cleanin' the horse pens, I'll ride up an' see if I can cuss him out for runnin' into the truck. We might as well have as much fun as we can with this."

"I'd like to be there when you do that," said Sally.

"We'll be in a little early, just be down at the horse pens. If he bumps the truck, you can cuss him."

The next day, as I rode to the horse pens, I saw Sally in the pen, talking to Bud.

"She's already cussed me out, Honey. You won't have to!" We laughed and got the dudes off their horses and made ready to have the noon meal. Sally even gave me a ride to the lodge in the golf cart.

The following day we gathered cattle and held another branding. Bud came out in the four-wheeler to watch. He was there early and carefully looked over the corrals.

We branded most of the day, only taking time out to enjoy the cook's barbeque.

After I'd counted the cows out, I gave Bud my figures.

Bud said, "I got here early and looked over the corrals. They need cleaning and Dwight and I are planning on doing it."

"Dwight an' you?"

"I haven't consulted with Dwight yet, but we'll do it."

I could see Bud's spirits were high.

"If you come out here, bring some extra diesel with you. I imagine you'll probably want to smooth out the four-wheeler trail," I said. "I'll tell Dwight where he can spread this manure. I've got a spot in mind that's a lot closer than where he's been putting it."

"I thought I'd do that," said Bud. "Great minds do think along the same lines!"

"If you don't get done, send Dwight back in the truck for the four-wheeler. You can leave the Skidster here overnight."

"You're just a regular thinking machine aren't you, Honey?"

"Probably," I said.

Pat, Chuck, Dwight, the dudes, and I left for the ranch. On the way back, I asked Dwight, "Are you gettin' tired of helpin' Bud? I can send Chuck out for a few days if you are, or I could help him."

"No," said Dwight. "I kinda enjoy the old man. He's fun. But I do miss riding my filly."

"The rest won't hurt her," I said. "Besides that, I don't want you ridin' her much more."

Dwight looked surprised. "You don't want me riding her. How come? Is there something wrong with her?"

I thought I'd have a little fun with Dwight. "Something wrong with her! Why, there's a lot wrong with her!"

Dwight asked, "What? Is it serious?" he was becoming concerned.

"It's very serious," I said. "Serious enough that I don't think you should be ridin' her!"

"What is it?"

"Take a good look, Dwight. Your little filly is pregnant!"

"You mean I'm going to be a father, that is, she's going to have a colt?" Dwight was clearly excited.

"You'll be a father before I am," I said. "I figure she's about two weeks away."

"Oh my gosh! What'll I do?"

"Don't do nothin'," I said. "We'll turn her out an' let her do it herself. She'll be fine."

Pat had ridden up beside us. "How does it feel to be a new father, Dwight?"

"I ain't a father," said Dwight.

"When that filly foals, be sure an' let Honey here know what it's like to be a new father. He's never been one before."

We all laughed and rode home.

When we got to the ranch, Dwight unsaddled his filly and turned her loose with a pat on the neck. "I'll be watching out for you, sis," he said. "You'll get a couple of weeks off."

"It'll be easier to help Bud knowing I can't ride my filly," Dwight told me.

"If you get tired of haulin' that manure, just let me know. I'll spell you or get Chuck to do it."

He said he was comfortable and I told him where to start spreading the manure when they started cleaning the branding corrals.

The Cleanest Ranch in the Country

The next day Bud and Dwight started cleaning the branding corrals. Dwight told me later that Bud was late showing up; he'd made some improvements to the four-wheeler trail.

Pat, Chuck, and I took out the dudes. We moved some cattle into a new pasture. I got to thinking that we should ride fence and make sure everything was all right. I didn't want to use Matilda as a pack animal to carry the fencing equipment, as the younger kids were having too much fun with her.

I asked Pat, "What if we used Einstein as a pack animal tomorrow to fix fence? The change of scenery certainly wouldn't hurt him an' we broke him to lead last winter. He's had a saddle on."

"He can handle it," said Pat, "although he might be a little barn sour. You lead him out an' I'll make sure he follows. Chuck can kinda keep the dudes out of the way in case we have to get western with him."

"We'll do it, if the little kids don't mind too much."

The next day we saddled the dude horses and I put a small pack saddle on Einstein. We loaded the fencing equipment and started out. I had Chuck lead the dudes out ahead of us, just in case we did have some trouble.

Einstein didn't want to move, so I gave him a hearty jerk on the lead rope and Pat moved his horse toward him. Einstein decided it might be easier to cooperate than resist and he followed right along.

Bud and Dwight left, with Bud driving the four-wheeler. They'd left the Skidster at the corrals. Dwight drove the truck.

We rode fence most of the morning. There wasn't much fixing to do, just a few sagging wires that we tightened up. On the way back, we met Bud and Dwight. Bud was improving the four-wheeler trail and was so involved in what he was doing he didn't even see us.

I rode closer to him and finally got his attention. He turned off the machine.

"You're like a kid with a new toy with that Skidster," I said.

"I've noticed a lot of little things that have needed being done for some time. Now that I've got the proper equipment, I think it's time I did them. Did you see the branding corrals? They are as clean as they've ever been."

"We didn't come by the branding corrals, we just saw you an' wondered what you were doin'."

"As you can see, we're working pretty hard."

"Keep it up," I said, grinning. "We're goin' to go get some dinner."

"Tell the cook we might be a little late getting in, but we'll be there."

We were just finishing the noon meal when Bud and Dwight came in.

"We'll have to go back for the truck," said Bud. "Dwight couldn't bring in the truck an the four-wheeler at the same time."

"I'll tell you what," I said, "let's give Dwight the day off an' you an' me will go back for the truck."

"That's okay with me. I'll be ready after I eat."

"Good. I'll tell Dwight he can have the rest of the day off."

I found Dwight and informed him of our decision.

"Do you mind if I get a horse and go out and look for my filly? She didn't come in this morning with the other horses."

"I noticed she was missin' this mornin'. You can take any of the dude horses an' go look for her. I'll come back with the truck that way an' keep an eye open for her. She might be off foalin' although I didn't think she was that close. If you find her, just leave her be. If she has foaled she needs a little time to get acquainted with the youngster."

Dwight caught a horse and headed out. I waited for Bud and when he was ready, we left in the four-wheeler for the branding corrals. On the way out Bud said, "When we get to the corrals, I want you to see how clean they are. And notice how smooth this trail is. I could make a four-lane highway out here if we wanted one."

"I will make a point to notice the corrals. Remember, we don't need you goin' around tearin' up the countryside with that Skidster. You know, this might be the cleanest ranch in the country. I think the only way it could be cleaner would be if you followed the cows around and collected the manure as they deposited it!"

"Now there's an idea," said Bud, laughing. "I'll take it under consideration."

We got to the branding corrals and I told Bud, "Your corrals are spic an' span. But I ain't eatin' my meals off them!"

Bud laughed and I could tell he was pleased and proud of his work.

I told him, "I'll be goin' back by way of the saddle horse pasture to help Dwight look for his filly. She's probably off foalin' somewhere, but I told him I'd look for her on the way back."

"You know, he is a good kid. I'll see you at the ranch later." Bud left in the four-wheeler.

I went to the manure spreader truck and started toward the

ranch via the saddle horse pasture. It wasn't long after I got in the saddle horse pasture that I noticed a saddled, riderless horse in a far corner of the pasture, so I headed in that direction. Soon I saw Dwight, crouched behind some sagebrush.

He was watching his filly nursing a newborn colt. I stopped the truck and walked over to where Dwight was crouched.

"You found 'em, huh."

"Yeah. How do they look?

"They're all right. What you hidin' for?"

"She didn't want to let the colt suck. I didn't want to scare her. I thought if she saw me, she'd run off and leave the foal."

"There's a lot of color on that colt. Can you catch your horse?"

"Yeah, I've got him hobbled," said Dwight.

"Let's just leave 'em here. They'll be all right. It's gettin' close to suppertime. We'll bring 'em in tomorrow. Let's go."

"Yes sir," said Dwight.

I waited until Dwight caught the horse then went to the truck and headed toward the ranch. I watched Dwight in the rear view mirror as I drove away. He was riding slowly, looking back at the filly and her colt.

As I drove toward the ranch, I met the saddle horses on their way out to graze. I stopped for a minute to watch them. They were in good shape, they were holding up well. The guide horses had been used the most and they were showing it a little, but they were doing well. I thought I was lucky, Sally had asked me to ride her two horses and that would take a lot of pressure off Roman and Drygulch.

I drove into the corral and Bud was in the Skidster scraping the corral, even though he'd just cleaned them a day or so before.

"Park it here while I load this little bit," said Bud.

"You just cleaned this corral a couple of days ago. What are you doin?"

"You said it," said Bud. "The cleanest ranch in the country! Soon as I load this, you can park it. I'm thinking we ought to do this more frequently!"

As soon as Bud dumped the bucket, I pulled out of the corral, parked the truck and closed the gate behind Bud as he left.

"Did you find Dwight?"

"Yes, he's comin'. His filly had a foal, there's a lot of color there. What are you goin' to do with her?"

"I'll just give her to Dwight. He's come to think a lot of her."

"What about the foal?"

"The colt should go with his mother," answered Bud.

That matter was settled.

The next day Pat, Dwight, Chuck, and I ran the horses in. Dwight was late as he went after the filly and her foal. By the time he got to the corrals, we'd had breakfast and had started saddling horses. Dwight put the filly and foal in a separate corral and started helping us saddle horses.

"You better get some breakfast," I told Dwight.

"I better help here," he said. "I was late."

"We can handle this," I said. "There's no need to go hungry around here."

The new foal caused a lot of interest among the guests and everyone had to take a look at him. Some guests took pictures of the new mother and her offspring.

Dwight left to eat and returned in time to help get the dudes on their horses. "I'm glad you let me eat," he said. "I was hungrier than I thought. Bud told me I was supposed to help you out here today.'

"Becomin' a father does increase a feller's appetite," said Pat, grinning. "Your new colt has caused a lot of commotion with the guests. I think you need to ride alongside the dudes so you can answer all the questions."

"I'll be glad to do that," said Dwight.

We did our riding that day, just a scenic ride, and the new mother was the main topic of conversation. Dwight did a good job of answering the questions and keeping the dudes satisfied.

August arrived and the warm weather got warmer. It was also dry. We hadn't had rain for quite a few weeks. Our horseback rides were stirring up a lot of dust and many of our guests declined to ride in the heat and dust. They spent a lot of time around the pool. Bud was concerned about the lack of rain.

"We'll have a tough time of it next year if we don't get some more water," he said. "And all that manure we spread won't do any good unless it rains. The grass is liable to be pretty short. The fishing won't be any good either."

About three times a week, Bud and Dwight were taking guests fishing. They were having a lot of success and ended up releasing a lot of fish that they'd caught. Bud was being more careful in the four-wheeler, he hadn't got stuck since Sally and I pulled him out earlier in the spring.

We held a branding about every week. The calves were getting big enough that we had to team rope them and stretch them out to get the branding done. Dwight wasn't much of a roper, but Chuck was pretty fair. Pat or I had to be on the ground doing the branding, ear marking, castrating, and vaccinating. Consequently, we didn't get a chance to rope together. I missed Sally at this time. She was a good roper and we made a good team and had a lot of fun.

Sally was present at the all the brandings, having come out in the golf cart. I tried not to show my frustration at Dwight's lack of roping skills, our brandings were taking too much time, but Sally noticed.

"Don't worry Honey, we have nothing but time. The longer we take, the more the guests like it. Next year, I'll be able to help out and it will be much better. And remember, the more these guys rope, the better they're bound to become."

"I suppose you're right," I said. "But I do admire good cowboy skills. Look at Pat, he's not showin' any frustration at all."

"Pat's good at hiding his emotions, especially in front of the guests. Remember, he's been doing this a long time, a lot longer than you."

Each day when we were done with our daily chores, Dwight was down at the corrals handling his foal. Chuck was generally with him and it wasn't long before the colt was halter broke and getting used to being around people. A lot of the guests went down to watch.

I watched them frequently. They were doing a good job. I told them, "Get real good at that, we'll have all our colts to mess with this winter. Don't forget to be pickin' up all his feet, that really helps."

Dwight asked, "All his feet?"

"Yes," I said, "but not at the same time!"

We laughed and I left.

One day Bud took me aside after supper and said, "I got a letter from the Forest Service today. Because it's so dry, they want us to pull our cattle off the forest land about two weeks early. There's no way we can fight it. I think we need to get the rest of our calves branded and get them on the forest land as soon as we can and take advantage of the feed that's still up there. Hopefully, that will leave a little more feed here."

"That means we'll need to get our cattle home by the third week in September, right?"

"That's right, Honey. We'll have to gather early. We'll also need to get a lot of extra hay to make it through the winter. I can call our hay suppliers and get the hay delivered if you want."

"You better do that," I said. "You know those guys an' can probably get a better price than I can. We'll schedule a branding for Monday. That will give us time to move the cattle that are here closer to the branding corrals. Do you think we might want to cull a little deeper this year? Feed is liable to be pretty short."

"We may have to," said Bud. "But let's see what the fall brings."

"We'll have guests at the ranch," I said. "A full day ridin' on the forest land, gatherin' cattle might be too much for 'em."

"We'll have to have Dwight or Chuck take care of them while you and Pat and whoever's left gather the forest land. It might be a rough gather, as dry as it is, the cattle will be scattered. I could maybe take some of the guests fishing, that might relieve a little of the pressure."

"I've noticed you ain't passed up many chances to go fishin'. I guess we'll manage somehow," I said. "I'll start adjusting my plans. Because of this, do you want to sell our calves earlier? We might not have the weight, but might do better on the price before the market gets flooded. Think about it an' let me know.

"By the way, I put an ad with the employment office for a woman to help out with the maid duties. If the employment agency calls an' sends someone out, will you handle it? I want to take some of the pressure off Sally an' we can't expect Missus Abercrombie to work."

"I'll take care of it," said Bud. "You're liable to be pretty busy right directly."

"This is liable to mean you won't be able to use the Skidster as much. Are you afraid of losing the 'Cleanest Ranch in the Country' title?"

Bud smiled. He'd been cleaning the horse pens on a regular basis. "We'll get around that somehow."

I told Pat of the changes required by the Forest Service.

"I guess there's nothing we can do about it. The one thing that's constant around here is that there's always change. Better get used to it," I said.

Being informed of the change in our plans, I started planning our adjustments with Pat. I looked over Sally's reservation board for September. She had done a good job, we were almost full. That meant we wouldn't have any room to house the cattle buyers in September. We'd have to sell our calves in October, about two weeks early.

With our accommodations almost full in September, that meant we'd have to gather cattle and handle dudes at the same time. That meant a lot of riding for Pat and me. Dwight and Chuck would pretty much have to handle the dudes. It also meant that we'd have to sort the calves off the cows with the dudes present. That might present some problems. Sometimes too much help is worse than not enough help.

If we didn't have any dudes riding, we could use both Dwight and Chuck as we gathered. We might have to try and convince some of the dudes not to ride. That idea didn't sit well with me; it was contrary to our purpose of being in the dude business. I didn't quite know how to handle the situation and decided we'd just let things play out as they may.

I thought about calling my dad and seeing if I could borrow my brother Tommy to help gather. I decided against that idea, Dad would probably be gathering his own cows and would need Tommy. I made up my mind that Pat and I would just have a lot of long, hard riding ahead of us.

The following Monday we branded the rest of the calves. We were finally done branding, that was one headache we wouldn't have to worry about. It was somewhat of a relief to be finished with the branding and as we turned the cattle out on the summer range, I thought it would be nice to give the other grassland a rest.

As we took the dudes out on a daily basis, I closely surveyed the grass situation. Having to bring the cattle in early would bring a lot of pressure to the pastures and what grass was left. The rest we were giving the pastures now would help. I tried to put these concerns behind me as I interacted with the guests.

The guests were oblivious to the ranch concerns. We tried as best we could to keep them happy and busy if they wanted to stay busy. Dwight and Chuck did a good job of intermingling with the dudes—they were far more outgoing than I was.

One morning at breakfast, Bud said, "I got a call from Scott last night."

I interrupted, "Scott?"

"Yes, Scott. You remember him, he worked for us for a spell last spring, and then quit. He wanted to know if we needed some help with our fall gather."

"What did you tell him?"

"I told him I'd have to talk to you."

"Well" I said, "he quit us early an' we were sorta countin' on him. While we still could use some help, I'd rather not have someone around who thinks he can come an' go at will."

As I said this, I looked around the table. I saw Pat nodding his head in agreement. Dwight and Chuck just looked at me.

"Good! That's my thinking exactly," said Bud. "He's supposed to call back in a little bit and I'll tell him we've got plenty of help."

There was an underlying message there and as I looked at Dwight and Chuck, I could see they got the message. I figured we were probably set for the winter.

Pat, Dwight, Chuck, and I left for the barn. As we walked to the barn, Pat and I lagged behind Dwight and Chuck. When Dwight and Chuck were out of earshot, Pat said,

"You made the right decision about Scott."

"He probably only wanted to work for a few days then go off to some rodeo. There was an underlying message there, do you think they got it?" I pointed toward the two hands ahead of us.

"I think so. But I don't think you have to worry about those two. They're pretty solid."

94

Rough Riders

We stayed busy during August, and it went by faster than I wanted it to. New guests arrived and they were satisfied when they left. Periodically I checked the reservation board for the following year. It was filling up. Sally had booked us more than half full for the following year

Bud was really pleased. "We've never had this many reservations for the next year before. You're turning this into a regular business, Daughter!"

Sally was pleased. "I'm glad Honey thought of the board and I'm glad business warranted getting one for next year. This little plan is really paying off. We'll have to be careful though, when we're full, we're full. My plan is to look at this year's figures, see what we have lined up for next year then consider adding another cabin or two."

"Don't get in a big rush, Daughter. Building a few more cabins is quite expensive."

"I know Daddy, I know. That's why we're going to look at all the figures, then make a decision! Remember, we're thinking a couple of years down the road."

Toward the middle of August, our reservations started to dwindle. We still had enough guests to keep us busy, but the tourist season was winding down. A lot of families were done with their vacations and making preparations for their kids to start school.

Bud hired a woman from town to come in and help out with the maid chores. Her name was Debbie and she'd had experience cleaning and making up rooms in the past. When she saw Sally's condition, she understood why Bud had hired her so late in the season. She also understood that her job was temporary, lasting only until the end of September or first part of October. We'd give her a room, meals, and a wage. She seemed satisfied with that and did a good job.

Although it was slowing down, we still managed to stay busy. I couldn't help thinking about our having to gather our cattle early and being short-handed. I thought the end of the tourist season might go a little easier because there wouldn't be so many kids, but it seemed like the guests that were around were a little more demanding. I laughed; it looked like I was in a no win situation.

I'll have to admit I was a little discouraged. I don't know if it was because we were losing some time on the forest land or if it was because it looked like Pat and I had some fairly hard riding ahead of us. It may have been that I knew we had a big job ahead of us and I wanted to get started. There wasn't anything I could do about it, I just had to accept it and deal with it as best as I could.

As the business slowed down in August, I started enjoying the rides with the dudes. We were almost full in September and I watched Sally's board closely. If there was any change, it was just to add more people.

I continued to take Sally to town for her checkups. These trips did provide me with a little relief from the dudes and I actually started to look forward to them.

On one trip to town, I told Sally, "I'm really concerned about having to gather cattle early. If we don't get 'em all we could be fined or even lose our permits. It's a fairly serious situation."

"I really wish I could help you," said Sally. "But I'm too big now to ride. Don't worry, Daddy says it will all work out like it's supposed to."

"I hope so."

September arrived and from the activity at the ranch a person would never know it was slowing down.

I asked Sally, "Where are all these people comin' from? There's more people here than you've got on your board."

"The people that are here that aren't on the board are just staying here one night. We're letting them stay one night and providing breakfast in the morning. People are calling it a bed and breakfast. We're actually charging more money on a daily basis than we do for our weekly rate. If any of these people want to ride, we'll charge for that. And if they want to make a reservation for next year, I'll be ready."

"What are you chargin' for the horseback riding?"

"I haven't figured that out yet, nobody's shown any interest," said Sally. "But, I'll charge plenty, you can bet on that."

"You're really goin' after the dollar, aren't you?"

"That's how success is measured these days," she said. "Besides that, we're a growing family, it won't hurt to have a little extra money hidden away."

I was going to tease Sally a little by saying she was the only one growing in this family, and she already had something hidden away, but thought better of it and didn't say anything. I thought she looked uncomfortable enough already and I didn't want to make things worse.

One night at supper, Bud said, "The Forest Service called today. They've moved the date we need to be off the land to the twentieth of September."

"I thought that was the original date," I said.

"We actually had until the end of that week. The twentieth comes earlier. We're losing about a week. You might want to start around the fifteenth, just to be on the safe side."

"We'll be ready," I said. "I won't guarantee that we'll have all our cows by then, but we should have most of 'em."

"I know you'll do the best you can. That's all we can expect."

The next day I checked the shoes on my horses and Pat's. I called the horseshoer and had him come out and reset the shoes on our horses. We'd be busy enough; we wouldn't have time to shoe a horse if a horse threw one.

On the twelfth of September I was leading a ride back to the ranch when I noticed a solitary horseman in the distance headed toward the ranch. He had a pack horse and an unsaddled horse following him. I was curious as to who he was and what he was doing. I got our riders to the ranch and watched him approach as we got our guests off their horses. He didn't ride to the lodge, but came straight to the barn. I thought I recognized one of the horses; he was a dun I had started a few years ago.

The rider got off his horse, tied him and the other two at the hitch rail. I had just put a saddle on its rack when I heard Pat say, "Well, hello Rod! How you doin'?"

I came out of the saddle room to see Pat shaking hands with Rod, Bud's brother. I went straight over to him and stuck out my hand. "It's good to see you, Rod. How you been?"

"Its good to see you both," said Rod. "And I've been good. Busy, but good."

"What brings you over this way? You're a long way from your own range," I said.

"I'd heard you were being asked to get off the forest land early and you were short of help. I thought if you fed me, I might be persuaded to help you."

"You heard right about being told to get of the forest land

early," I said. "An' you were right about bein' short of help, but you know we'll feed you. You don't even have to work! How'd you hear about gettin' off the forest land early?"

"Fred let me know. I guess the Fish and Game is part of the Forest Service. Fred hears a lot being the game warden. Well, I'm here to help out if you want. I even brought my own horses."

I asked, "Is that the dun I started a few years back?"

"Yes, and he's a good one. Tough as nails."

"He's filled out nicely an' growed some. Unsaddle him an' your pack horse an' turn 'em in with ours, there's plenty of feed for 'em. Put your stuff in the bunkhouse or take it to the lodge. You can stay wherever you want. I know Bud will be glad to see you. Who's watchin' your sheep?"

"I've got three Mexican herders with the sheep. They do a good job."

There was a fun family reunion at the lodge that evening. Rod hadn't seen Bud since the wedding.

Sally was surprised to see her Uncle Rod. She had no idea he was coming. She gave her uncle a big hug. She asked him, "Why are you here?"

"It's a good thing I came," he said. "You're in no condition to ride." He turned to me, "What do you mean, putting your best hand out of commission like that?"

I didn't have an answer for him and he teased both Sally and me mercilessly that evening. I became a little embarrassed, but Sally stayed right with him and they engaged in a friendly and fun bickering.

Rod and Bud stayed up quite late discussing old times and what was happening in the cattle and sheep business now. I got tired and excused myself and went to bed. Pat had left earlier. I had stayed up past my bedtime, but I slept good knowing that we had some extra help and good help at that. As a youngster, Rod had ridden all this country gathering his father's cows.

The next morning at breakfast, I got with Bud, Rod, and Pat and discussed the plans for gathering the cattle. "I thought we might leave real early an' take the truck out to the forest. I think we can save some time that way. As we come in, one of us can load his horse an' bring the truck in. We'll do the same thing the next day. If we ride the creeks first, we can make a pretty easy gather each day. The cattle will be pretty much scattered, the hard part will be gettin' those cattle that are way out."

Knowing that both Bud and Rod knew the country better than I did, I asked, "How does that sound to you? You got any suggestions?"

"We'll just have to see how things go when we start," said Rod. "Who else are you going to take? We should have at least four to make it work good."

Missus Abercrombie had been listening. "You wild cowboys seem to forget that I'm here and can still ride. I have every intention of helping you."

"Virginia," said Bud. "I had no idea you were planning on going! That's going to be a pretty rough ride."

"It will be easier than in the past. Honey is going to taxi us out in the truck, remember? That's a luxury you never gave us in the past, Bud Wilson!"

"That will still be a long ride back," said Bud. "Are you up to it, Virginia?"

"It may not," said Rod. "We can put the cattle outside the Forest Service gate and leave them. If we do that each day, we can bring all of them home at the same time. The older cows will start to drift back toward the ranch anyway. That way, we'll have more time on the forest land and we can cover more ground."

"You see, Mister Wilson," said Missus Abercrombie, very sarcastically, "it won't be as rough as you have made it in the past. I'm looking forward to it."

"We may have a plan," said Bud.

"We do," said Rod. "That's what we'll do. Does that sound good to you, Honey?"

"It sounds like we have a plan," I said, although I had very little to do with formulating it. I was learning that it was easier to be foreman by letting the help direct, to some degree, their actions. I was finding out that it wasn't necessary to exercise my position of authority to get things done. By allowing the help to voice their opinions, we were getting things done and we had some good, even better ideas to consider.

"Are you going to take Dwight or Chuck?" Sally had been present during our discussion although she hadn't offered any suggestions.

"I don't know," I said. "We'll have to see what develops and then make a decision."

We left to make preparations for the day's dude rides. Rod didn't join us; Bud took him in the four-wheeler and gave him a tour of the ranch, pointing out the improvements we'd made since he'd been here. He was here for the wedding, but with all the things that were going on then, there wasn't time to show him around.

I was glad Bud had taken Rod for the day. It would give his horses a few days to rest. I knew he was a hard rider.

The following night, I made sure Pat and I kept in the horses we were going to use for our first days gather. I also kept Missus Abercrombie's and Chuck's horses in. I'd decided to take Chuck on the gather and let Dwight handle what dude rides we had. If we didn't have any dude rides, he could accompany Bud in whatever he did.

I wanted to get an early start and told Pat, Rod, Missus Abercrombie, and Chuck that we wanted to have breakfast about four in the morning, saddle up and be moving by five.

That would put us at the Forest Service gate around six and we could start gathering cattle. They all nodded in agreement and everyone went to bed early.

The next morning, I was up early. I saddled Drygulch for myself then saddled Missus Abercrombie's horse. Pat, Rod, and Chuck were up soon after and saddled their horses. Dwight had also gotten up and came to the barn to see if he could help.

Missus Abercrombie was already up and eating breakfast when the rest of us came to the kitchen. "You boys are running a little late," she said as we entered the kitchen. I didn't know if she was serious or just kidding us.

"Maybe so," I said, "but your horse is saddled an' ready to go. Soon as we eat we'll be gone."

The cook came around and handed everyone a paper sack. "There's something to eat," he said. "You might get a little hungry out there today."

We grabbed our lunches and went out and loaded our horses in the two-ton truck. I looked over the situation and said, "Missus Abercrombie, you come with me. I think it will be a little crowded with all five of us in that truck. You an' me will take my truck. You'll have an opportunity to start this cow gather in style!"

"Some style," she said as she got in my truck.

"Well," I said, "we could have brought the manure spreader truck."

The lady just grinned at my comment and I thought to myself, *She ain't such a bad ol' gal after all.*

Pat drove to the Forest Service gate and we unloaded the horses against a bank.

"Pat," I said, "why don't you an' Rod make a big circle out to the west? Chuck, you an Missus Abercrombie make a smaller circle around to the south an' west. I'll …"

"I don't need a babysitter," interrupted Missus Abercrombie.

"I'm not givin' you a babysitter," I said. "After you an'

Chuck get out there a ways, you're goin' to split up. You will be responsible for bringin' all the cattle here. Chuck will make a bigger circle an' you pick up what cattle he sends to you. I'm givin' you the easiest circle, but it's the most important part. Towards afternoon, you an' Chuck look to the west. When you see the cattle Pat an' Rod have gathered, you can go out an' help them. Or, if I make it back before them, you can come an' help me. I'll be comin' from the east. Bring everything, even if it's the neighbors' cows. Be sure an take the lunch the cook fixed for you. Any questions? If not, let's get goin'."

We started out, the riders going in the appointed directions. I headed out toward the east. I had given myself a pretty big circle, but felt confident I could cover the ground. I passed some cattle along the way and started them back toward the gate. I doubted they'd make it to the gate and made a mental note of the area they were at. I'd have to check it on the way back just to make sure they made it to the gate.

I was a little surprised at how many cattle I found. I had thought they would be more scattered than they were. I got quite a ways away from the gate and was still seeing more cattle. Around one o'clock, I ate the lunch the cook had fixed. I didn't see any more cattle off to the east and decided I'd better start back. I had no idea how many cattle I'd started toward the gate and I hoped they all kept heading in that direction once I'd started them.

I started pushing cattle. I'd start them, get them moving good, and then leave them to get other cattle. I did have the advantage of the Forest Service fence on one side. That cut down the riding I had to do to keep the cattle moving in the right direction.

I don't know how far the cattle had strung out, but I had quite a few cows heading toward the gate. It was tough on Drygulch, pushing cattle toward the fence, then going back and bringing up the stragglers, then going out and pushing cattle toward the fence. Each time I went out, I'd look and see if I had missed any cattle.

Drygulch was getting tired and so was I. The cattle had stirred up a lot of dust and the sweat on Drygulch had turned the dust into mud. It had caked on him. "Keep it up ol' Partner," I said, as I patted him on the neck, "I'll give you a good brushin' when we get done tonight." I noticed when I patted Drygulch, that I was covered with dust also.

Soon, I noticed a couple of riders headed toward me from the south. I couldn't tell who they were, but they were pushing little bunches of cattle toward the larger herd I had gathered. I was grateful for the help.

As they approached me, I recognized Chuck and Missus Abercrombie. They put the cattle they had with the ones I had and we stopped to visit.

"Who's watchin' the gate?"

"Bud came out with Dwight in the four-wheeler. They're watchin' the gate and trying to get a count on everything. They've also brought some cold lemonade in a cooler for us. I think we've left enough for you."

"Good," I said. "Have you seen anything of Pat an' Rod?"

"No," said Missus Abercrombie. "There have been very few cows come from that direction all day. You've sent more cows to us than they have."

"They're probably bringin' a big bunch all at once," I said. Secretly, I hoped so.

We moved the cattle toward the gate. I had Chuck do the out riding. His horse was fresher than mine and I thought he could gather the cattle that may have holed up in some of the little draws and gulches. I had Missus Abercrombie riding along side the cows. She could help Chuck as he brought cows to us.

We soon reached the gate. Dwight was turning the cattle into the gate while Bud was counting them. When the last cow went through the gate, Bud called me over.

"There's some lemonade here for you, Honey."

I rode over, got off Drygulch and had some lemonade.

"Your horse looks like he's worked today," said Bud.

"Yes, he's really earned his keep today," I said. "Seen anythin' of Rod or Pat?"

"Nope. There's been a few cows come from the west every now and then, but there's been no sign of Pat or Rod."

"There's some cattle comin' from the west. I think we ought to ride over there an' check it out. I'll take my other hands here an' go. Are you up to more ridin' Missus Abercrombie?"

"Certainly, young man. Do you think I'm goin to shirk the most important job here?"

I noticed Bud trying to stifle a laugh.

"If you're ready, we better get goin'. Come on Chuck."

We circled around the approaching cattle, pushing them toward the gate. I saw the two riders, separated by a big distance, one of them pushing the stragglers, and the other riding alongside. From this distance, I couldn't tell who was who.

I had Missus Abercrombie drop away from Chuck and myself, telling her, "Just keep 'em goin' along the fence. Don't crowd 'em too much."

As we approached the outrider, I recognized Rod. "Dwight, you give Rod a hand here. I'll go back and help Pat."

From the looks of Rod's horse, he'd put in a busy day. I rode back to Pat.

"Need a little help here?"

"It sure wouldn't hurt none," replied Pat. "How many you figure we got here?"

"I don't know. Bud an' Dwight are gettin' a count back at the gate."

"How'd you do?"

"I don't know," I said. "I forgot to ask Bud before I came to help you. Looks like you got more than I got. My cattle were strung out so far, I couldn't tell. I think we've got more than half of them. We'll get the figures when we get to him. Your ol' pony looks like he's been used today."

"We've put in a pretty tough day," said Pat. "It don't look like your horse has been on a picnic."

"It's been a pretty tough day all the way around," I answered.

"Before I forget," said Pat, "I want to tell you what a good job you did with Missus Abercrombie this morning. Telling her she had the most important job here was a stroke of genius! Rod and I laughed all the way out here until we split up. I don't think she'd have lasted all day out here."

"Probably right," I said. "She's still thinkin' she's got the most important job; at least that's what she said when we came out here to help you. I've got her up front, just keepin' the cattle movin'. Sometimes I think she might have an over inflated idea about her value. But she's a pretty good old gal."

"Yep, I'll bet she was something when she was younger."

We pushed the cattle toward the gate. I moved ahead so I could slow them down as Bud counted them going through the gate.

When they were all through the gate, Bud said, "It looks like we've got about sixty five percent of them! That's better than I thought you'd do; I thought you'd be lucky to get half of them. That's the best gather we've had in a long time. Rod, you, and Pat better get some lemonade. It's still cold."

Pat and Rod got off their horses and got a drink. They hadn't had anything to drink all day.

Missus Abercrombie said, "That's what happens when you give a woman the most important job! This young man here, Honey, he knows how to get things done!"

Bud gave Missus Abercrombie a funny look. Pat whispered, "I'll tell you later," and Bud let it drop. But he still had a puzzled look on his face. We loaded the horses and went back to the ranch. When we got there, it was after dark.

"Virginia," said Bud, "Dwight here can take care of your horse. Come to the lodge with me and tell me how your day went."

We took care of our horses and I gave Drygulch a good rubdown. Then we selected the horses we wanted to ride for the next day's gather. I picked the big paint that Bud had given Sally as a wedding present. I didn't know if Missus Abercrombie was going to ride tomorrow, but kept a horse in for her. I also kept a horse for Dwight. It would be his turn to help gather tomorrow; Chuck could help Bud.

We all went to the lodge to eat. Sally met me at the door.

"Where are you going?"

"To wash my hands an' face," I said.

"Oh no you're not! As filthy as you are, you're going straight to the shower! The cook can hold supper another fifteen minutes."

Upon hearing Sally give me my orders, Pat, Dwight, and Chuck silently left for the bunkhouse to get a shower. Rod went to the room Bud had given him in the lodge. I went to our shower.

Cleaned up properly, Sally allowed us to enter the lodge and eat.

At supper, I lined out the next day's plans. They were pretty much the same as the day before. We'd get another early start and do the same thing again.

"Virginia, I think you'd do better going with me in the four-wheeler. You've had a pretty rough day. And you can still be out there."

I noticed both Pat and Rod smiling as Bud made his comment. Missus Abercrombie must have filled him in as to how important I apparently thought she was to the operation. I even had to smile a little.

Missus Abercrombie reluctantly agreed, looking at me for support. "If you think it will still work out," she said.

I nodded, but was afraid to say anything.

The next morning we saddled fresh horses, loaded them in the two-ton truck and left. Once again, the cook had fixed us something to eat for a noon meal. I took my truck again and followed the two-ton, thinking it might be a little more comfortable for everyone, especially on the way back after a hard day riding.

When we arrived at the gate, there were four cows and calves standing on the Forest Service side of the gate.

Rod asked, "How'd we miss them yesterday?"

"I don't know, but we won't miss them today," I said, as I opened the gate. "Those cows must want to go home pretty bad. They might have an idea of what's happening." The cows went through the gate and headed toward the home range.

We unloaded our horses and I instructed the riders to cover the ground we didn't cover the day before. Pat and Rod left. I took Dwight with me.

Dwight filled me in on Bud's activities the day before. "He made me bring him out here," said Dwight. "He told me he hasn't missed a fall gather all his life and was too old now to start missing them. It's all right, isn't it?"

"Sure," I said. "After all, he owns the place. He can do whatever he wants."

We got out away from the gate. I'd noticed some cattle in the distance. I pointed them out to Dwight and said, "When you come back, make sure you swing around that way an' pick up them cows. I'll go around the other way an' get what I can get. About one or two o'clock, start headin' back an' bring everything. We'll meet at the gate. I think Bud will be at the gate again along with Missus Abercrombie."

We split up and started hunting for cattle. Today's ride would be tougher than yesterday's, as there were fewer cattle to find and I was sure they would be more scattered.

I decided I'd go up one ridge and come down another. Being higher, it would give me a better look at the country. I could see Dwight about a mile away. It looked like he had already found some cattle. I couldn't see Pat or Rod, but there was some dust off to the southwest. They'd either found some cattle or had stumbled onto some mustangs, I couldn't tell which. I hoped they had found some cattle and weren't chasing wild horses.

I made it up the ridge I was traveling, checking the canyons on both sides without seeing any cattle. It was pretty steep and I had to give the big paint a few chances to catch his wind. I decided I'd come down another ridge and check the canyons on both sides of the ridge. This might save some time and miles.

I wasn't having much luck finding cattle. I thought it would be quite humorous if I, the foreman, showed up without any cattle. I would never live that down, especially if everyone else brought cattle in. It could become an embarrassing situation. I did have to laugh at the thought of it.

I finally found some cattle in the bottom of one canyon. Before I started down for them, I checked the canyon on the other side of the ridge thoroughly and didn't see anything except a few elk.

I started down toward the cattle I'd seen. There wasn't a trail and it was some fairly rough traveling. I tried to stay out of the timber. I didn't know how much downed timber there was.

I heard some movement ahead of me and couldn't tell if it was cattle or elk. I was hoping it was cattle. The noise sounded like it was headed the right direction.

Coming out of the timber, I saw the hind end of some elk headed into the next patch of timber. I couldn't see the cattle I'd come down here to get and hoped they were headed in the right direction. I thought I'd get just a little more height and see if I could spot the cattle. I headed up the side of the mountain, and caught sight of the cattle headed off to the southwest. If they went west it was all right, but going south was not good, so I urged the big paint into a trot in an effort to turn the cattle more northwest. It was tough going and we had to take the long way to get ahead of the cattle.

After some hard riding, I got ahead of the cattle and turned them the way they were supposed to go. I stayed on the cattle and kept them moving at a good trot. They kept wanting to go back south, but the big paint and I kept them together and headed to the northwest. I sure didn't want to lose the only cattle I'd seen all day.

I would have liked to have checked the next ridge, but didn't trust the cattle to keep moving in the right direction.

I kept the cattle moving and soon reached Dwight. He had a lot of cattle and they were moving the right direction. The cattle I mixed with them were content to slow down and travel with the rest of the herd. They had gotten a little tired. Dwight and I visited a little as I let the big paint catch his breath.

"How come you got more cows than I got, Dwight?"

"Just a lot of hard riding," he answered. "Some of them gave me a rough time."

"There's another valley I'd like to check back there. The cattle I mixed with yours gave me almost too much to handle. I was afraid to leave 'em for fear I'd lose 'em. Can you take these cattle in while I check it out?"

"I think so."

"Just take it slow an' easy," I said, "an' you shouldn't have any problems. I'll check out that valley an' catch up to you. Don't lose 'em, no matter what you do!"

I heard Dwight say, "Yes sir," as I rode off at a trot. I thought I could give that valley a quick look and get back in good time.

The big paint covered the ground to the valley in good time.

We went half way up on the side hill where I could get a good look at the valley. I saw some cattle at the far end and stayed on the side hill until I got around them and could get them started in the right direction.

These cattle were more cooperative than the first bunch I found and I didn't have any difficulty starting them in the right direction. They didn't want to move very fast and I just let them go at their own speed, encouraging them when necessary.

When we came out of the valley, I could see the dust the cattle Dwight had were creating. I hurried my cattle in order to catch up. From all the dust that was being stirred up, I thought Dwight was having problems.

When I got to Dwight, I saw that Pat and Rod had met him with the cattle they'd gathered. They weren't having any problems; they'd just gathered a lot of cattle. Combined, we'd gathered a lot of cattle that day.

I stopped to visit with Pat and Rod and let my horse blow. From what they said, I was the only one that had any problems with cattle that day. I also came to the conclusion that I had found the fewest cattle that day, but I didn't say anything about that to anybody.

When we were done visiting, I moved to the head of the herd and kept them pointed in the right direction. I could also slow them down if Bud was at the gate counting.

I was relieved to see the trucks and the four-wheeler at the gate. Soon we would be done. Another day of hard riding was almost over. I got to wondering if the dude rides weren't letting me get soft rather than toughening me up.

Bud was counting the cows through the gate. When he had his count, he said, "You boys have done better than I expected. According to my count, we have three more cows here than what we turned out! I don't think I've added wrong."

"We might have some of the neighbors' cows," I said.

"That's possible. I wasn't high enough to see all the brands on the cows as they went by. We'll get a count when we gather to preg check. There's lemonade here if you want it. You fellers might be kinda dry."

We all got a drink, loaded the horses, and headed back to the ranch. On the way, I told Dwight, "We can ride through the cattle with the dudes the next couple of days; we'll look for any of the neighbors' cows we might have brought in. It'll give the dudes something worthwhile to do when were ridin'."

Bud was satisfied that we'd completed our gather. I wasn't quite sure. Even though we had a couple of days of some pretty rough riding, it seemed too easy. I was hoping I was wrong, it would be nice to have it completed. I did go over my figures and compare them with Bud's. They added correctly and they should have, as I'd given my figures to Bud.

Marketing Time

The next day Pat, Dwight, Chuck, and I took the guests out through the cattle, looking for the neighbors' cows. We didn't find any. I thought we'd have to ride through them again.

Rod and Bud spent the day visiting. Rod's plan was to give his horses a day's rest then go back to his sheep.

The following day, after a lot of goodbyes and a lot of thanks from me, Rod left. I didn't know when I'd see him again, but I sure appreciated him showing up when he did. We took the dudes out through the cows again and I did see one of the neighbors' cows. I recognized her; she was one of the cows that I'd found that wanted to go south.

I made a mental note of the cow and decided to call the neighbors when we preg checked.

"One good thing about havin' to gather early," I told Bud, "is that we got all our cattle home before the huntin' season starts. If you get some more signs, we'll ride around the outside fence an' repost it. I'm sure some of them were torn down by hunters. When do you want to sell calves an' preg check?"

"Do that the next time you take Sally to town," said Bud. "I'll let Fred know that we're posting the ranch again and encourage him to ticket trespassers. I'll call the vet and see when he can come out and do it. Soon as he does that, we'll hold our calf sale."

On our next trip to town, I picked up the signs. The doctor and Sally determined that she was about a month away from delivering. "It'll be around the middle of November, according to the doctor," she told everyone.

Missus Abercrombie said, "That's good. Sally and I will go to town around the first of November, check in at the hotel and we'll be ready."

"What?" I was annoyed that I was being left out of the deal.

"That's right," said Missus Abercrombie. "We will handle the situation in town."

"How come?"

"It's a long way to town and it might be snowing by then. The roads will be treacherous. I don't think we want that baby delivered in a car during a snowstorm by a cowboy!" Missus Abercrombie was very adamant about it.

"Virginia, you may be right," said Bud. "That might be the best thing to do for Sally and the baby, Honey." Bud directed his last comment at me, knowing I felt left out.

"Of course I am right," replied Missus Abercrombie.

"If you think it's best," I replied. I noticed Sally nodding her head in agreement. "I don't think I'll be very comfortable in town for a week or two."

"You don't have to stay in town," said Sally. "Missus Abercrombie and I can handle everything, with the help of the doctor, of course."

I was in a difficult situation. I knew I should be in town, but I didn't want to be. There wasn't that much to do at the ranch, but I felt I needed to be there also.

Sally saw my concern. "We can call you when things start to happen. There isn't much you can do there anyway."

The plan was made. Sally and Missus Abercrombie would go to town the first week in November and stay at the hotel. They would have the company car. They would call the ranch when Sally started to experience labor pains. The hospital was only four blocks away from the hotel.

"When we call you, you can call your parents," said Sally. It appeared that everything was already planned with out consulting me. I thought I would just do as I was told.

Bud had called the vet. "We're going to preg check next week. The vet will be here for two days and he'll be bringing a helper again. We'll give them a place to stay. We'll sell our calves the following week, the first week in November."

I told Pat of the plans that had been made.

"Women tend to take charge these things," he said. "They're better equipped to handle them. When you have to go to town, just go. Don't worry about anything here, Dwight, Chuck, an' I will handle everything."

"I'm thinkin' we ought to run in the broodmare bunch an' wean the colts," I said. "We can start halter breakin' 'em. We also need to gather the cattle an' get ready to sell the calves. Our calf sale will be the first week in November. We can gather the cattle, sort off the calves starting tomorrow. We'll need to pick our replacement heifers, sort off the Longhorn crosses, an' sort the heifers from the steers. This baby business has kinda got me off schedule a little, I'm feelin' rushed."

"We ain't rushed," said Pat. "We're right on schedule. You just feel rushed."

"I'm also a little confused," I said. "Let's get the cattle work done, then run in the broodmare bunch an' handle them."

"If you're a little confused, that's normal," said Pat. "It isn't every day that a feller has his first born."

"Don't be afraid to correct me if I make some mistakes," I said. "I do have a lot on my mind."

Pat laughed. "Don't worry. We'll get through it."

The next day we gathered cattle and separated cows from calves. We separated the neighbors' cows. Then we went about sorting calves according to sex. We had plenty of room in the feedlot to keep the calves. We turned the cows into a pasture that would be easy to gather when we preg checked. I had the feeling I was missing something but couldn't put my finger on it. We also selected some replacement heifers. We'd keep them in the feedlot and breed them artificially as yearlings to calves as two-year-olds. The program was proving to be a success.

Periodically, I checked with Pat. "Am I missing something?"

He'd just laugh and say, "No, just relax. We're doin' fine."

Concerned that I might be missing something, I said, "Let's not forget to feed them tonight. Remind me to call the neighbors about their cows."

Pat laughed some more. "Relax. We'll get 'er done."

The vet came and we got the preg checking done pretty much as last year. I did notice that we didn't have as many of the heifers we bred as yearlings cut into the "open" pen as we had last year. As usual, Bud was present and said, "It looks like your idea of a cleanup bull is paying off, Honey. We don't have as many open heifers."

"We'll be able to tell better when they calve," I said. "But it does look good now."

We had cut a few older cows into a separate pen. These cows might not make it through the winter. They were pregnant, but we were going to sell them rather than running the risk of feeding them through the winter and losing them later. "We might sell those cows at the sale," said Bud. "They're all pregnant and they might bring a better price at the sale than here."

I asked, "You don't think the buyers will be interested in pregnant cows?"

"No," replied Bud. "They're mostly buyers for feedlots and slaughterhouses. Unless they've got a special order for pregnant cows, they won't be interested. You can check with them, if you want, it won't do any harm."

"I'll do that. It might save us an extra trip to town," I said.

"The cattle buyers will be here in two days," said Bud. "I haven't invited as many as other years; I'm getting a little tired of providing room and board for a lot of buyers that don't buy or even make a serious offer. We'll save a little there, in money and time."

Our sale day arrived and the buyers arrived the day before. They spent the afternoon looking through the calves, open cows, and the old pregnant cows. I stayed down at the corrals close to the pregnant cow pen just to answer questions about the pregnant cows if necessary. There weren't many questions, but some buyers did show some interest.

It rained the day of our sale. We provided rain jackets for those buyers that didn't have them. Either Pat or I accompanied each buyer, one at a time, into the corrals. They'd look over the calves then I'd send them to Bud to make their proposals. We did it with the steers then we did it with the heifers. Then we went into the Longhorn-cross steer pen, then the Longhorn-cross heifer pen. When we were done with the calves, we went to the open cow pen. Then we went to the pregnant cow pen.

I told everyone, "These cows have all been preg checked by the local vet. We'll guarantee 'em pregnant as long as the vet does." Everyone laughed at that comment.

"They've just got a little age to 'em an' we're goin' to move 'em now. It'll be a good 'two for one' deal if you have some pregnant cow orders to fill. If you're interested, tell Bud. We could split 'em up if you want. Take a good look boys, there's some good older cows there!" I was getting a little excited about the sale.

One cow buyer bought all the calvy cows, saying, "I have a feller who's trying to get started in the cow business. These cows might help him get a good start."

Our cattle sale was over. Bud let the buyers use the phone to call for their trucks and they could stay until their cattle left. The following two days were spent loading cattle into the semi's. I did feel a certain amount of relief when all the cattle were gone; our daily chores became a lot easier.

The next day, Pat, Dwight, Chuck, and I gathered the broodmare bunch and ran them in. The colts looked good—there was a lot of color. Bud was at the corral with Sally when we arrived with the horses.

"I think we'll keep the mares in for a few days. I want to look them all over. We may sell a few in the spring. If we keep any fillies, we'll need another stud. I don't want too much inbreeding in my horses."

"It'll just be easier to halter break 'em," said Pat.

"We can start playin' with the colts now if you want," I said. "We can run in the yearlings and comin' two-year-olds tomorrow an' start playin' with them. We've got a little slack time."

"There's no rush," said Bud. "Sally and Virginia will be going to town next week. We don't know when you're going, let's see if anyone wants a few days off while we've got the time. Dwight or Chuck might want to do some hunting. There's still a few days of the season left."

As it turned out, Both Dwight and Chuck wanted to go hunting. "Why don't you take a couple of days and go? Pat an' I can handle everything here."

"We were wondering if we could just take a couple of horses and hunt from here. We really wouldn't even have to leave the ranch," said Dwight.

"Of course, if we got anything, we'd bring it back here. The ranch could use it," volunteered Chuck.

"Don't you want to go to town or anything?"

"Not really," said Chuck. "I've got about everything here that I need." Dwight agreed.

"Do what you want," I said. "Take today an' the next two

days. We'll expect you to be back in three days. If you get anything, be sure you bring it here as fast as you can. As warm as it is, it won't take long for it to spoil."

Sally had packed a suitcase for her stay at the hotel before going to the hospital. With Missus Abercrombie's help she also packed a bag for the baby. She also packed a bag for me, just in case I had to spend more than one day. Sally put her bag, Missus Abercrombie's bag, and the baby bag in the trunk of the company car. She left my bag by the door of the bedroom so I wouldn't forget it.

At the end of the first week in November, Missus Abercrombie announced, "Sally and I are going to town this afternoon and get settled in the hotel. Sally or I will call each night around suppertime and let you know what's happening. When she has labor pains, I'll call you from the hospital."

The plan was laid out and Missus Abercrombie set forth the plan just like a general giving orders to his troops.

This came as kind of a surprise to me. "I don't see the need to go now," I said, "what little snow we've had hasn't stayed. We've had a really warm fall."

"You're bound and determined to deliver this baby in the calving sheds or the pickup, aren't you, young man?" Missus Abercrombie seemed to be very adamant about going to town. I could see there was no sense in trying to convince here differently, and decided to keep quiet.

Sally and I said our goodbyes about two that afternoon.

"You call when you get to town an' let us know that you made it safely," I said.

"You bet," said Sally. "Don't you be doing anything foolish while I'm gone. And when you come to town when Missus Abercrombie calls, take your time. Don't drive foolishly or recklessly. There's nothing you can do when you get there anyway."

"Yes ma'am," I said and gave her a kiss. She returned the favor and got in the car.

"It won't be long now," said Bud. "Pretty soon you'll be a father. Congratulations, my boy, congratulations!"

That night Sally called. They had made it town safely and there wasn't anything going on.

Dwight had got an elk, a big bull. I thought he was old enough and would be tough enough that we should make jerky out of him. The cook agreed.

"We'll have enough jerky to provide all the guests with all they want all summer long," he said. "I can make it up in my spare time."

Two days later, we got our first major storm of the season, about a foot. It continued to snow the next couple of days, not steady, but snow showers. When Missus Abercrombie called that evening, she sounded quite pleased that she and Sally had gone to town early and out-foxed Mother Nature and me!

Three days later when I came in for breakfast, Bud was already up, having his coffee.

"Mornin', I said as I poured me a cup. "You're up early."

"Good morning," said Bud. "And congratulations! You're a father!"

"What!" I was surprised and I almost spilled my coffee.

"Yes, you have a new baby girl!"

My first thought was, *What do we want with a used baby girl?* I sat down.

"When? What? I thought they were supposed to call."

"Virginia did call, around two this morning," said Bud. "It all happened so fast, the baby was born while she was on the phone. She called me back and told me not to wake you, there wasn't anything you could do. I was surprised you didn't hear the phone. It was her and Sally's wish that you come today; they thought it would be a lot safer on the roads. It's snowing in town."

"I'd better go to town," I said. "There's not a lot to do here. Do you want to go to town with me?"

"I think I'll just wait here," said Bud. "You kids need some time to get acquainted with your new daughter. Call Sally before you go."

"I'll get cleaned up then call her. She's probably asleep now. Two o'clock this morning, huh? Maybe we should have been feedin' her only in the evenings, like the cows. She might have had the baby at a more decent hour."

Bud just laughed.

I got cleaned up then called Sally and told her I was coming to town. I was ready to meet my new daughter.

Other Books by Stu Campbell

Horsing Around a Lot

Horsing Around the Dudes

Humor Around Horses

You Can't Be Serious!

Comedy Around the Corral

More Humor Around Horses

A Young Cowboy's Adventure

Honey

Surprise!

Intruders